Introduction to the Cabala

D1300901

Introduction
to the
Cabala

TREE OF LIFE

by

Z'ev ben Shimon Halevi

SAMUEL WEISER, INC.

York Beach, Maine

First published in 1972 by
Samuel Weiser, Inc.
Box 612
York Beach, Maine 03910-0612

Revised edition, 1991

99 98 97 96 95 94
9 8 7 6 5 4 3 2

ISBN 0-87728-816-X
CCP

Cover art is from a 16th century woodcut by Paulus Ricius

Printed in the United States of America

The paper used in this publication meets the minimum
requirements of the American National Standard for Per-
manence of Paper for Printed Library Materials Z39.48-
1984.

For
Rachel

Acknowledgements

I would like to thank every person who, consciously or unconsciously, living or dead, has contributed to this work. Particularly, I am grateful to my forefathers and to various personal mentors, especially those in the tradition of the Society of the Common Life.

Contents

Illustrations

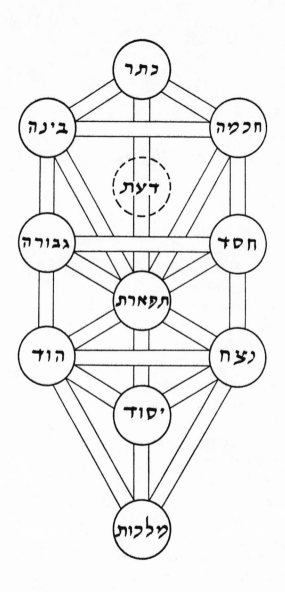

Preface

The Cabalistic Tree of Life has been with us for two thousand or more years. Every age has seen it through its own eyes and this book is an attempt to cast it into twentieth-century terms so that its blossoms may flower for another season.

The Tree of Life is an analogue of the Absolute, the Universe and Man. Its roots penetrate deep into the earth below and its top branches touch the uppermost heaven.

Man, meeting point between heaven and earth, is an image of his Creator. A complete but unrealised Tree in miniature, and lower than the angels, his is to choose to rise higher by climbing the branches of himself, and so gain the ultimate fruit.

London 5731

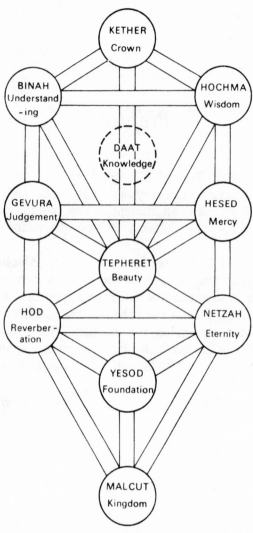

Tree of Life

I

Introduction

The Tree of Life is a picture of Creation. It is an objective diagram of the principles working throughout the Universe. Cast in the form of an analogic tree it demonstrates the flow of forces down from the Divine to the lowest world and back again. In it are contained all the laws that govern and their interaction. It is also a comprehensive view of man.

The relative Universe hovers between two poles. All and Nothing. Either end of this fluctuating axis may be seen as Nothing or All, as both become the entry and exit points for the Absolute who stands apart from Creation. Here we have the full reality. All else is, to the ultimate observer, illusion —a cosmic drama composed and dissolved in a cyclic round of plays within plays from the subtlest reverberations in the Highest worlds to the slowest movements and changes in the coarsest Materiality.

The Absolute has no direct contact with creation yet Being permeates through the matrix of the Universe, supporting it like the silence behind every sound. Without this negative reality nothing could come into existence, as shadow can not manifest without light. Here in the relative world we move amid particles and waves never for the most part suspecting that what we touch is always disappearing, and what we see is not really there. Solidity is a charade, a temporary state of nothing, frozen for a time into a form that is familiar to us, who are ourselves but travellers in the ever changing scenery called earth.

Creation is separate from its creator even more than a modern production of *Hamlet* is far removed from Shakespeare. Yet creation bears its Author's hand and though the actors may interpret, the play remains essentially as the Master conceived it. The relative Universe, like our analogy of a play, is constructed in the same design with protagonists and supporting cast set against a series of backgrounds in which different roles, seeking to find equilibrium, create and operate dramatic events known as evolution.

The relationships between the various actors or forces is very precise, though they may take up different attitudes under specific conditions. This set of combinations is laid out in the Tree of Life so that a given situation may be examined and its participants and their true status be revealed.

The Tree is a model of the relative Universe. It is the template of all the world, carrying within it a recurring system of order. Moreover any complete sub-organism or organisation is an imitation of its plan. Man is the prime example. He is a microcosm of the macrocosm. His being is an exact replica in every detail in miniature of the cosmoses above him. True, he moves in the physical world, is made up of atoms, molecules and cells yet he partakes in the subtle realm of forms, can assist in conscious creation and has access to the Divine.

As man is an image of Creation so Creation is but a reflection of the Creator. By this resemblance we are able to study that which is below by looking at that which is above and that which we cannot observe above by examining that which is below. Through the Tree of Life we have an objective connection which gives us insight and knowledge by the principle of parallel—into the upper and lower, inner and outer Universes.

In our account the origin of the Tree of Life is traced, then the power of its illumination and formulation. Following the development of its conception we see that cosmic principles apply to any whole entity. Observing its workings we are shown how the tree gathers into an intelligible order all aspects of phenomena and demonstrates them in a reflective picture, a Universe wherein the Creator is present even in the densest of matter.

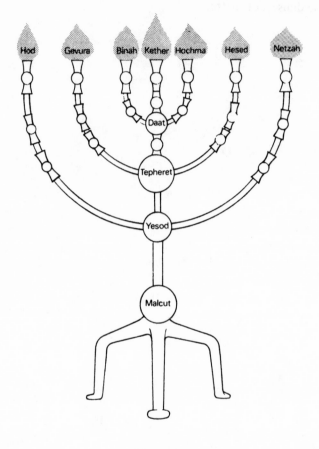

Menorah

II

History

The actual origin of the Tree of Life is unknown. It traditionally is rooted in the Cabala, the inner teaching of
Judaism. All complete religions have two faces. The outer
facet takes the form of words and public ritual, while the
inner aspect is the internal, often an oral instruction which
is passed on from teacher to pupil, who face to face have a
personal rapport in which the Master knows what and when
it can be taught to further the disciple's development. When
the pupil becomes a master in his own right he in turn im-
parts his own wisdom and understanding to the next generation; so that without a break a Tradition may be carried on
over several thousand years, without a trace of its outward
appearance.

This oral method is common to all the major religions.
However, like many human institutions, it is subject to
decay and corruption so that from time to time in history
there is a reformulation of ancient objective principles
adapted for the language and customs of the current day.

It is said that Abraham the father of the Hebrew nation
received the original Teaching from Melchizedek, King of
Salem, who was also a priest of the most high God. The
name Melchizedek means 'King of just men' or 'my King is
righteousness', and Salem, the ancient name for Jerusalem,
means 'peace'. This may be seen as historical fact or allegory,
for the Bible can be read as an outer or inner account of
events which take on the form of living parables.

Prior to this happening, Abraham had come to the conclusion, after deep research in contemporary religions, that
there was only one, invisible, living God. Now after being
initiated by Melchizedek, matched to this belief was the
introduction to objective knowledge, an understanding that
out of the creative fountainhead of God came many manifestations, and that these were not to be mistaken for the
Creator. Abraham knowing that he was known by God made
a pact with Him to pass the knowledge on. This was the
Covenant.

The Hebrews retained this understanding with their
Maker over many generations, though occasionally they lost
sight of it when their tradition was adulterated by neigh-
bouring customs and beliefs. The essence however was
periodically revived as when Moses dragged a half-reluctant
slave-minded people out of the symbolic, as well as literal
land of Egypt into a spiritual rebirth. In the desert of Sinai a
whole generation of old slave habits had to die off before a
new Israel could be set on its original direction.

Without doubt objective knowledge about the Universe
was held at the time of Solomon for it is written into the
biblical text of the period and the construction of the Temple
and the seven branched candlestick are both formulations of
the Tree of Life, as were the columns Jachin and Boaz on
either side of the Temple veil. The physical diagram of the
Tree built into the Temple was lost when this first Temple
was destroyed and the Jews taken into exile in Babylon.

In Babylon strange events occurred. Besides Ezekiel's resur-
rection of Israel's religious tradition, which urged them to
return home to Jerusalem, the men responsible for the inner
teaching of the Religion realised that here was a unique
possibility at the second rebirth of the Nation. Hebrew, in
the over-riding presence of the vernacular used in Babylonia,
had ceased to be a first language. So here was a chance to
embed, before it became established again as a national

speech, many ideas—make it a language that contained more than just an everyday vocabulary of meanings. At this point we know that the actual twenty-two letters of the alphabet were reconstructed, changed from the ancient pictograms into a more robust alphabet known as the Syrian script.

Later, long after this new Hebrew had been established, (though it never quite took over from Aramaic the lingua franca of the Middle East), it became regarded as a holy language, and like Sanscrit to be used in Holy matters.

One work in particular reveals the philosophical construction of the Hebrew alphabet. This was the Sepher Yitzerah, reputed to be written by Abraham, but more likely to have been drafted in the earlier centuries of the common era. In this, to each letter was ascribed a planet and a Sign of the Zodiac. Herein lies our date clue in as much that the Sign Libra was inserted into the Zodiac circle long after Abraham died. Other qualities were attached to each letter, and the whole pivoted on a system of the three creative principles embodied in Air, Water and Fire. Here the various combinations of these three forces made the Universe function, and numerous arrangements of letters and their corresponding numerical values described the positions and relationships evident in the macrocosm of the world and the microcosm of man. Drawing possibly from Greek sources it also used the Pythagorean concepts of a triangle or trinity containing the ten letters relating to the name of god. Scholars disagree as to who formulated this diagram first.

The interchange of objective knowledge between wise men of different nations and traditions during the few hundred years before Christ was more common than is generally supposed. Intelligent men obviously met and exchanged ideas while their fellows fought over trade and politics. The Jews, though often considered a particularly insular group, were no exception as far as the perceptive thinkers amongst them were concerned. While Pythagoras travelled the eastern Mediterranean in search of knowledge, no doubt Rabbis, though not of the merely learned kind, also sought wise company—even in alien cultures. In the seaport of Alexandria founded by the Greeks a great library devoted to the nine muses was set up. Here at this first museum were gathered ideas from all over the known world. To this remarkable centre, one of the early Ptolemies invited seventy Jews so that the Hebrew books he had heard respectful reports of might be translated into Greek. With these scholars no doubt came Rabbis versed in the Cabala, the inner explanation of the Bible. These men probably made connections with the inner teachings of Greek and Egyptian philosophy and religion and from this cross pollination more discoveries were added to the distinct traditions. There is much evidence of shared ideas in Greek thought and an uncheckable fable has it that the Tarot cards, which appear in mediaeval times, trace back to the wall diagrams in the corridors of Egyptian temples. These cards on close scrutiny show more Greek and Hebraic thinking than Egyptian symbolism.

The adding of new ideas and reformulating of old ones was a feature of the Cabala Schools, and rabbis down the centuries have hammered and tested every addition before its inclusion into the body of Cabalistic literature. The test of argument, along with the flash of enlightenment, kept a balance necessary for the narrow path of vision through the forest of illusion. For this reason men were not allowed to study the Cabala until their full maturity, lest the wine of mysticism overbalanced them like a drug trip to the modern young. A man had to be experienced in life, have the stability to handle and master the things of earth before he could attempt the portals of Heaven.

It is said by some scholars that the first writings on the Cabala were set down in the second century of the common era by people present at the discussions of Rabbi Simeon ben Yohai. It is maintained by other scholars that

many if not all the books of the Zohar commentaries were
written or compiled by a twelfth-century Spanish Jew, Moses
de Leon, whose widow claimed he wrote them to make
money under the blind of their being ancient works, because
people then, as now, like and value antiques. This does not
matter. More important was that the Cabala emerged into
the open and we get in mediaeval Spain, which took over
from the decaying authority of the Babylonian rabbinical
school, the full diagram of the Tree of Life.

Besides its effect on the golden Arab-Jewish era in Spain
the Cabala and its ideas had a powerful influence on Christendom. The Church was at that point in need of reassurance
for its more intelligent clergy, who were being disturbed by
the quality of ideas coming from Muslim and Jewish universities and were consequently finding that Faith was not
enough. Helped by others, Thomas Aquinas the Catholic
scholar found the solution in his study of Judaism, which
combined the cabalistic work of Dionysius the Areopagite
with that of Aristotle. Out of this he was able to formulate a
whole theology which was later to be grafted into Church
teaching. Contrary to the platonic Christians he brought the
abstract universe into the mundane, relating God and angelic
influences through the Tree of Life to the world of elements,
plants, animals and men. Out of this Cabalistic concept came
the nine orders of the church hierarchy. Even the great
cathedral builders were influenced. Erected by the masons,
who based their ideas on the Temple of Solomon, the west
front of each church had two towers representing the twin
columns on either side of the Temple veil. Here were the two
outer columns of the Tree of Life, the masculine and feminine aspects, the active and passive forces, flowing down
from Heaven. Called, in Chartres cathedral, the sun and
moon towers, this idea is repeated in later centuries though
the source reason is forgotten. Another concept is the Holy
Trinity of Father, Son and Holy Ghost, with the Cabalistic

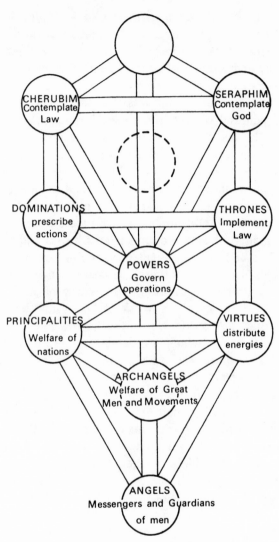

Tree of Thomas Aquinas

Bride represented in the rose window of submission. Looked at with a knowing eye many cathedral plans take on a new meaning.

By Renaissance times the Cabala and the Tree of Life were known to many scholars. The Zohar, with its complex of studies on the Bible, numerology, angels, the nature of man and many other allied subjects had been printed, and gentile scholars took much interest, partly to relate it with the knowledge coming in from the Byzantine world and partly because of its relationship with magic. This application of the Cabala brought it into much disrepute even amongst the Jews themselves, for it gave rise to occasional mass psychosis and outlandish movements in certain northern European Jewish communities who desperately needed some mystical straw to hang on to during the recurrent waves of persecution.

This magical side, mostly misunderstood or fractionally digested, both fascinated and repulsed men who came in contact with the Cabala. To the genuine scholar and philosopher it was a Jacob's ladder up to Heaven, a method of study, the basis of a righteous code and a point of reference upon which to relate contemporary art and science. To the charlatan and the aspiring professional Messiah it was a magical weapon to cajole, frighten and fascinate individuals and groups. Like twentieth century technology, it could be made to work for or against man, lifting him out of the mire of drudgery or destroying his soul and body. At one end of the scale cabalists discussed the nature of the Universe with Pico della Mirandola, brilliant light of the Medici court, at the other end Cabalistic amulets were sold to keep off evil spirits or injure enemies. Popular Cabalism reached its height in the seventeenth and eighteenth centuries with a surfeit of Messiahs and mystics all of whom, except one, disappointed their followers. This one saint, Israel Baal-Shem, a natural mystic, was the focus of the Jewish revival movement called the Hassidim who flourish to this day. However, much of this Cabalism was based on visions and wonder working, and while Judaism received a much needed impetus, the movement was more related to the parallel revivalism then going on in Christendom than to philosophy. Hassidism thrived, though not without resistance from the orthodox Rabbis, even to the point of Baal-Shem's excommunication. In time this great thrust of energy lost force and became formalised and institutionalised by custom rather than by spontaneous conviction. However, the so-called Cabalistic practices still continued, so that even amongst the nineteenth century Jewish immigrants from eastern Europe to the west, there were to be found Cabalists who would make charms to offset the evil eye.

This degeneracy of outer Cabalism did not however hinder the researches of thoughtful Jews and Gentiles. Work was still carried out wherever the Cabala and Tree of Life were intelligently considered. Most of this effort was of scholarship, a blend of the intellectual detective with a dash of hope that some key might unlock the mystery. Many books were written and ideas developed but none of the quality of the middle ages and earlier. The seventeeth century produced many speculative contributions, but by the nineteenth century the natural sciences had begun to interest thinkers more than mysticism.

In the nineteenth century in the West various semireligious movements, composed of people disappointed in materialism and their own formal religion, arose. These groups also included Jews who felt that orthodox Judaism did not fulfil their philosophical needs. Rabbinical discussion had become mere learned argument. There was no longer spontaneous wisdom and understanding or real interest in the inner meaning of Judaism, especially when Jewish intelligence became involved with the concept of Zionism.

Gradually the objective of Jerusalem shifted from the spiritual to the practical, and politics took over from polemics. Zion, the yearned-for home of the exile, changed from man's seeking to regain Eden into the reinstatement of a nation in Palestine.

At the present time Judaism, like all formal religions, is losing its hold on the younger generation. However, this does not mean our time is irreligious. Far from it. Many of the young are seriously looking for meaning in a complex and conflicting world situation. Many people are at this moment involved in seeking out the truth through drugs, and others belong to esoteric groups studying numerous systems and methods. Many of these organisations are based on the oriental approach and are sometimes quite alien to the Western temperament. While it is argued that these give a fresh outlook the effects of this adulteration occasionally divide a man, creating spiritual conflict. One cannot mix traditions and cultural temperament so easily. Every philosophy and religion is peculiar to its own place; moreover the English hippy in Katmandu is half way between not only East and West, but ancient and modern times. Here lies a dangerous limbo so often entered by quite sincere people. In the West we have our own traditions, just as old as the East and as well tried. Cabalism is one of them and an integral part of the Judaic-Greco-Christian tradition of Europe.

This then is our brief. The Tree of Life, as the name implies, is concerned with the living word. It exists now, in the twentieth century, as well as in eternity. Our task is to transcribe the Tree into modern idiom so that it becomes manifest for us and others. Unless the top Sephira of Kether is connected with the bottom Sephira of Malcut the Tree of Life is incomplete—and Heaven cannot reach Earth.

III

Negative Existence

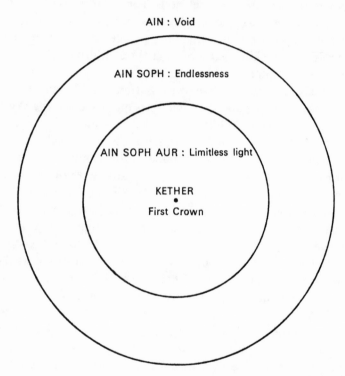

AIN : Void

AIN SOPH : Endlessness

AIN SOPH AUR : Limitless light

KETHER
•
First Crown

There is an Absolute and a Relative Universe. Between them lie the veils of negative existence. The Absolute is beyond even eternity. It is timeless, without form, without substance —beyond existence. It is nothing and everything. It undergoes no change yet is not changeless—it just is.

The relative Universe is the manifestation of Creation, the

unfolding of a divine impulse, a vast seedbed coming into flower, then fruit, which on completion decays, dies, and returns to its source ready to be born again.

Within this huge complex everything has its time and place, and though some features and functions appear on vastly different scales of size and lifespan everyone fits precisely into a whole, as our sun fits into the scheme of the Milky Way, and a liver cell relates to our body. Superficially the substances of the Universe may appear to be similar, but the water of the sea, for instance, is not the same as that of a pond, nor can it support the same kinds of life. It is the relative position that alters its function. Moreover a molecule of water, continuing the example, may pass through many states. First as vapour such a molecule may be buffeted in a cloud. Then after falling within a drop locked on to a nucleus of dust, it becomes one of millions in a puddle that seep into the earth, before being absorbed by a plant. For a time it may be fixed in the organic structure, part of the juices which in turn are sucked out of the plant fibres by an animal. There it flows in the blood stream of the creature until perhaps that animal is killed and eaten by man. Here again the molecule passes through many diverse experiences in the human body until it is excreted. Having got this far it passes through the various mechanical, chemical, and organic processes of a sewage works before being released into a river where it flows with a myriad other molecules of water, all with quite different tales to tell, back to the sea. There it might spend several centuries in the depths before being convected up to the surface and evaporated into the atmosphere as cloud again. This is the relative world in miniature.

In the relative Universe it is a question of time and position. The sun is young middle-aged in comparison to most stars and the earth is still adolescent with its first growth of green hair on its face. Mankind, by its general performance, is probably in its childhood—judging by its periodic tantrums and breaking of toys! All is relative, each level fitting into the one above and containing the one below, the whole fitting into a grand design from the highest and most potent energy down to the densest of elements. Here we have the top of the Tree of Life, Kether—the Crown—and the bottom, Malcut—the Kingdom.

The Tree of Life defines the relative Universe at all levels. It is the archetypal pattern. However, above it, beyond Kether—the Hollow Crown through which the Creator manifests—lies the unmanifest of negative existence.

Negative existence is the intermediary zone between the Godhead and his creation. It is the pause before the music begins, the silence behind each note, the blank canvas beneath every painting and the empty space ready to be filled. Without this non-existent Existence nothing could have its being. It is a void, yet without it and its potential, the relative Universe could not come into manifestation.

Negative existence is ever present on all levels of creation. It lies behind space and time. Without it there could be no galaxies or men. It contains, as a room's space does—the void we live in. Emptiness is the still background time moves against. Negative existence enables a man to be what he is. Mirror of Mirrors, Negative existence's non-interference allows the most perfect reflection of Creation.

The veil nearest to the relative Universe is Ain Soph Aur—the Limitless Light—that is, that which is everywhere and penetrates even the thickest matter, as do certain cosmic rays which are so fine they pass clean through our planet as physical light does through a pane of glass.

The second veil of which we know even less is Ain Soph—the Limitless. This is the first step towards manifestation of the Creator. It is the point where Ain the Ultimate void begins to focus out of Nothing into the Limitless or endlessness, where there is something that is, at least, endless.

Beyond this there is—NO-thing—and beyond that, the Absolute. These three stages constitute a condensing, a crystallising out of the Being who permeates the whole of All; of a point in the centre of a circumferenceless sphere. This distillation, this point, is without dimension either in time or space, yet it contains all the worlds from the upper-most realm down through the ladder of creation to the lower end which is composed of space, gas, galactic clusters, galax-ies, stars, planets, organic Life, man, organs, cells, molecules, atoms and the subatomic realms down to that zone where matter ceases to be solid and becomes first energy, then an illusive nothing again.

This all inclusive dot is called the First Crown, the first indication of the Absolute, perhaps better known as I AM, the first of many God names.

Out of this top Crown stream all the beings who have ever been, are, or will be. Contained in the negative existence be-yond lie myriads of possibilities. Man sees only a thin sec-tion of this ever present dimension. In him are all his children and his children's children. Out of Adam came all men. Did Abraham guess at the full meaning of his seed becoming a nation? No one except perhaps the wisest can perceive what lies within him, what is present at that point in a negative form, ready to manifest tomorrow or a million years from now.

This is negative existence, that which is there, but not there, that which by its very nature is the closest yet is the hardest to see. Here the Absolute is separate from his crea-tion, yet is ever present within it.

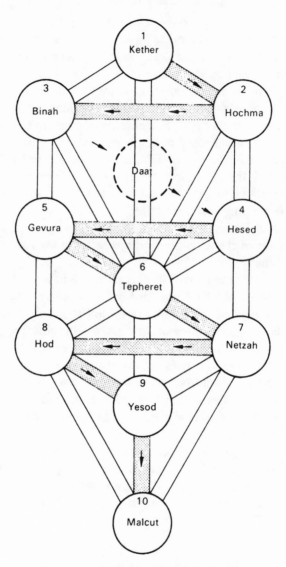

Lightning flash

IV

Lightning Flash

The structure of the Tree of Life is based on the emanations flowing down from the first Crown. After the initial impetus of creation a sequence unfolds from the first Sephira (or container) through eight stages to resolve in the tenth Sephira known as Malcut, or the Kingdom, at the bottom of the central pillar.

This prime development might be likened to a musical octave from Do to Do with each note fulfilling a particular function as the emanations interact between energy and form, as expressed by the right and left pillars of the Tree of Life.

This progression is known as the Lightning Flash as it zig-zags down the tree. Beginning with Kether—the Crown, it flows towards Hochma—Wisdom, where it manifests itself as a potent dynamic at the top of the active column headed by Abba the cosmic father, or male principle. It then crosses to Binah—Understanding, which as Aima the cosmic mother heads the female column. The active and passive columns are also called the pillars of severity and mercy, the latter being the male. Here the Trinity of Creation begins to function, as the divine energy out of perfect equilibrium seeks to find its level and resolve again. The flow of emanations, not diminished in essential nature, though transforming into another order, then crosses the central column of equipoise and passes on to the Sephira Hesed, or Mercy. Here the power, on being received into the active column again, takes on the dynamic expansive quality of this stage, before emanating across to Gevura, or Judgement, in the fifth station. Here the force is checked, balanced, and adjusted, before being passed on to Tepheret, the vital Sephira on the middle pillar of the tree. At this juncture there is a critical point of equilibrium. Tepheret, or Beauty, has a special relationship with Kether the Crown, by connection through the axis of the central column. The only thing that separates Tepheret from Kether is an unseen Sephira known as Daat, or Knowledge, which functions only in particular conditions. At Tepheret an image is held, it is a mirror of Kether, but operating on a lower scale. The emanations are then passed into the active Sephira Netzah, or Eternity. This is the point where active functions repeat and repeat to maintain the energy level. From this transformer the emanations cross to Hod—Splendour. This may be also translated from the Hebrew root word as Reverberation, which is perhaps a better description of the function of Hod, whose job is to pick up and pass on information. From here the emanations again touch the central column and focus on Yesod or the Foundation. Here they are again mirrored, but more dimly, being a reflection of a reflection, yet powerful enough to cast a strong projection—but only a projection. Directly below is the last Sephira, Malcut—the Kingdom. In this are accumulated all the energies, active and passive, and all the processes received from the Sephiroth above. This is the resolving Do of the completed octave.

The Sephiroth on the Tree might be regarded as a system of functions in a circuit through which flows a divine current. Each function creates not only phenomena, but transforms all the adjacent sub-circuits. Any Sephiroth can change the direction of flow, creating variable fields and actions. Power may be stepped up or down in all Sephiroth thereby modifying events, while the current returns to Source via the Earth of Malcut.

An example of the Lightning Flash passing down the Tree is seen in the process of writing a book. Kether is the Crown, the creative principle. The idea is conceived in Hochma. As a vision it can be very powerful, the seed of a great novel, but in Hochma it is merely an idea, potent but formless. Over a long period it will begin to formulate in Binah. Perhaps it is better as a play or a film? Maybe as a story, short and to the point? Time and the principle of the top receptive Sephira of Binah shapes it into a book of, say, medium length, centred on a particular situation in which certain characters will participate. At this stage it may be held for years in a writer's mind, perhaps never to be written. But one day it may focus into a definite entity with a grand design. This is Daat, knowledge. From that time on there begins a quite new process which is called 'cooking' by some writers. The incubation period is followed by the Hesedic or gestating action and has the quality of great growth and expansion. Situations crop up, fragments of conversation intrude into the writer's consciousness, characters begin to develop of their own accord, the whole story begins to fill out and overflow. It is at this Hesed point of the operation that the writer must get to work, or lose by sheer mental dissipation ideas welling up inside him. He begins to write an outline, setting down the creative forces present in him. However, he must continually judge and assess (the function of Gevura) what the Hesed gives him, for it is often more than he needs and so a constant editing comes into the action. Gradually the book begins to take form; the essence, or Tepheret, starts to show. Maybe it is the great work of the century, the distillation of a lifetime's experience, perhaps it is just a humble textbook on stage property-making, but it still has its stamp, its quite distinct quality. This is how we distinguish a Tolstoy from a Hemingway. In Tepheret the synthesis of form and energy is centred on the middle column, and here is the reason why this Sephira is known as Beauty. However, at this point the book is still hardly visible, it is mainly in existence in the mind of the writer. He has to set it down in its entirety, or it is just another unwritten masterpiece. Netzah, or Eternity, does this task. The vital forces of the body, controlled by Hod, the voluntary processes, make the pen move over the paper. Netzah knows its job instinctively while Hod, trained in mental and physical reflex, focuses the acquired knowledge or language into what will be intelligible sentences. Yesod, or the Foundation, which is an amalgam of all that has gone before, organises the whole operation in a personal style and reflects back what has been written, while retaining a memory image for reference. Malcut is the body and the book itself, the actual physical manifestation in the world. Heaven has reached Earth.

Here in this illustration we have a brief outline of the Lightning Flash as described in the Human Tree of Life. All creative processes in the Universe follow the same pattern, though in the terms of their own level.

V

Tree and Man

The Tree is said to underlie any complete being or organisation. How does it then relate to Man? For it is most important that one verifies knowledge directly with one's experience or it becomes merely learning.

Old engravings superimpose a human male figure with raised arms on to the Tree of Life with the column of passivity on his right. This differentiates the Microcosmos from the Macrocosmic Tree of Life which has the Sephiroth from left to right. In this way the Microcosm forms a mirror-image relationship with the Universe.

In these diagrams the Sephiroth are sometimes directly assigned to parts of the body: Tepheret the heart or solar plexus, Hesed the left arm, Gevura the strong right arm, Yesod at the genitals, with Netzah and Hod for the legs which stand on the Kingdom of Malcut or the Elements. Binah and Hochma are sometimes placed either side of the head, and in other diagrams in the palms of the raised hands, with Kether the Crown high overhead.

My own sympathy, however, subscribes to the school that places the whole physical body in Malcut with its vital processes circulating in the Netzah-Hod-Malcut triad, with the Sephira of Yesod acting as a reflecting screen of consciousness in its centre.

Beginning at Kether as the unknown full potential of man, we follow the Lightning Flash in its zig-zag path down through the being of man.

In Hochma—Wisdom, we find the function of the Inner

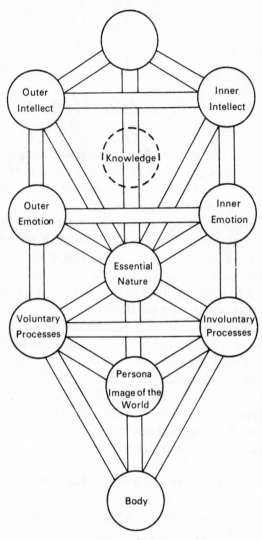

Tree of Man

Intellect. This is the deepest part of the mind, the highest intellectual centre from which emanates silent thought. From this potent area the most profound ideas and observations come. This centre sees with the inner eye of illumination, and speaks without words, as Wisdom. It has an almost divine quality, and indeed it has direct connection with the Divine World. Originality is its hallmark and in most men is only heard consciously several times in a lifetime. It is said that epilepsy, the divine disease, is the state produced when a man suddenly has an excess of Hochma and blacks out as the rest of his organism cuts off the blast of light. In the rare case it may manifest as a flash of genius, or the closing steps of Enlightenment.

Counterbalancing on the passive column is Binah—outer intellect or understanding. As the name implies this Sephira stands under and receives. It is feminine and responds as formulation to the active input coming across the Tree from Hochma, and down the path from Kether. It resolves by receptive intelligence the communications into understandable principles. This is a lengthy procedure sometimes taking many years. Einstein said that he saw certain ideas in a moment, but had to spend a long period working them out, to get back to the original conception. This time factor is a quality of Binah. Besides receiving from above, Binah also responds to the flow coming from below. Experience in the outer world accumulates in Binah as understanding and an event observed many times is seen in terms of an overall view. 'It always happens that way,' says the outer intellect. Constructively taken this is useful for seeing the grand design, but thoughtlessly used it constitutes a too generalised and conservative outlook. Here we see how emphasis on one side of the Tree or the other results in a reactionary approach on the passive column, or a revolutionary one on the active side. Neither are balanced, but must be centred on the middle pillar of equilibrium. Binah in this case acts as the counterpoise to Hochma, and vice versa. This occurs all the way down the Tree, each side checking the other. Binah is reflective thinking, to back up inspiration. It is method, the setting out of principle, the long view and the appreciation of cosmic processes and patterns. We see these two upper Sephiroth working in wise old men, and sometimes in the deeper parts of ourselves. In cosmic terms they are our father and mother both in physical and psychological, as well as spiritual terms.

Hesed is inner emotion, the quality of devotion observed in a lifetime's work, the depth experienced perhaps in one love affair, or the sense of feeling touched on in a profound religious moment. This Sephira in man represents a powerful creative urge, the kind of force that will make a people develop a continent, devote time and money to good works, give loving care to a demanding family, or spend conscientious attention on the practice of an art. It is the emotional mainspring, the deep-water current that a man draws on for resource, when ordinary emotions are inadequate. This is the place where magnanimity originates, and from where higher feeling rises up.

Hesed in man is another inner voice. It is not the valued judgement of Gevura—its outer emotional compliment on the Tree. Hesed has the quality of mercy and generosity; however, overbalanced it can become a deluge of feeling, a drowning love, a benign despot who sees his licence as a right, tolerating anything. In this unbalanced state a man dissipates his wealth and health in indulgence, his lack of Gevura or judgement allowing complete Laissez-faire. A little less extreme is the Hesed centred intellectual who will take up an over liberal position. He will quote, usually from a secure Hesedic material situation, ideals about universal freedom and the brotherhood of man, while his less fortunate fellows are oppressed by criminals taking advantage of his lack of vigilance.

Gevura—outer emotion—is the counterweight in the emotional pair of opposites. Its function, sometimes defined traditionally as Severity, is to judge from moment to moment as one does in everyday matters. Ideally Gevura should be impartial, but no man has this feature built in. It has to be created by the balance and interaction between the positive and negative sides of the Tree. This desire for equilibrium is sought throughout Creation in all worlds. It is also expressed in the Traditional name of the middle pillar of 'Clemency' which stands between the columns of severity and mercy.

With Gevura should come passive assessment. It receives the emanations from Binah above, and together with its own understanding forms a judgement, which according to the philosophy worked out or accepted by Binah, may range from the orthodox to the eccentric. Even an anarchist has his Binah and makes this his point of reference for his judgement. One only has to observe a heated political discussion to see Binah and Gevura at work.

In its relation to Hesed, Gevura works correctly as the feminine aspect. Like Binah Gevura responds also to the external world. Listen when meeting somebody new and you will hear your Gevura present an unvoiced critique on everything about them. Behind this is perhaps your forgiving Hesed, while above an often conventional Binah sets the background for the opinions. Of course these are very mundane reactions but for most of us they are the only ones we can easily identify as different parts of our psyche.

Gevura unchecked, that is without the balancing element of magnanimity from Hesed, becomes positively aggressive instead of receptively sharp. Uncontrolled it can turn a man into a bigot, a disciplinarian, or a cruel partisan. This is the Sephira of Aye or Nay, as a servant excellent, as a master militant and dangerous. In terms of larger human affairs it is the institutions which decide, under law—Binah—

what is right and wrong. In social reforms it is the forces that clear away hypocrisy and corruption. On the individual level Gevura destroys lies and disease—a vital function in any mind or organism. Overactive Gevura talks in the inquisition and McCarthyism, while the passive Hesed advocates licence in whatever field is being discussed, whether it is economics, ethics, social custom or the arts. Here once more emerges the necessary principle of reconciliation embodied in the middle pillar, sometimes also known as the column of mildness.

Tepheret—Beauty—is the focus of the essential nature of a man. It lies on the central column, the axis of consciousness which flows up and down from Kether to Malcut. In man, the height at which he is centred on this column determines the level of his being, and while the two columns on either side perform functions, the column of equilibrium shows what he is.

One's Essential Nature is that which a man is born with. It is his very own yet it partakes of the realms above and the kingdoms below. Tepheret has been described as Kether on a lower level, or in Biblical terms a man in God's image. Tepheret is that which is most real in an individual. Here at the focus of eight paths is the synthesis embodied in Tepheret. Known traditionally as the Judgement Seat it has access to all the Sephiroth except Malcut—the Kingdom— or in man, his body. That is why a man's essential nature cannot be seen in the physical world, though its character may be traced in his actions.

Tepheret, Beauty, or the Essential Nature of a man, is his consciousness of himself. He knows of himself, though he may forget it most of the time so involved is he in activity. It is the watcher in moments of great danger. It is the observer who sees without eyes, whose awareness marks moments with a strange lucidity. Here is what you are, a reflection of I AM.

Tepheret is called Beauty and not without reason. It is the point of equipoise, the perfect symmetrical centre of the Tree of Life. If you wish to examine any complete organism, place it on the slide plate of Tepheret, and the Tree will act as a microscope. Using this essential crystal all the aspects will find their places on the Tree, each Sephira demonstrating through its principle and function the structure and organisation of the thing you are examining.

In man his essential nature is his key. 'Know thyself' say all philosophers. In Tepheret is this self, poised half way between Heaven and Earth. Embedded in the body for a time it partakes of the upper and lower worlds, bringing the Divine down into Matter and raising matter up towards spirit. Tepheret is at the juncture of the visible and the invisible. When you meet a man you have not seen for twenty years, his physical appearance may have changed profoundly since you saw him at school, yet you recognise him without question. Is it the features? The eyes? No—it is something else, quite personal to him and even after eighty years still peculiarly his own. This is the Essential Nature shining out of the man.

This Sephira has a special place. It is a point into which things flow from all directions and flow out again, but more important upon it hangs the creature, for Kether can exist without the rest of the Sephiroth. Without Tepheret or a man's Essential Nature the body of Malcut would be a soulless automaton, a mere system of divine plumbing with no possibility of evolution. Tepheret then is the nodal point of growth; every lesson learnt is fed into the Seat of Judgement slowly raising its level from a dormant being into an active fully grown, awakened participator within the person. This is perhaps the meaning of the story of the Sleeping Beauty and all her slumbering court. As a Tree of Life we are the palace, the princess and all the courtiers, but where is the prince?

Above Tepheret on the axis of consciousness lies the invisible Sephira of Daat or Knowledge. Placed below the
Crown, it represents in man the point where he does not
just know of, but is. It is in this instant that his individuality
vanishes and he may experience—or non-experience—union
with the Divine Kether. At rare moments in meditation, we
are told such a phenomenon occurs. One vanishes not into
dreams as is mostly the case, but into nothing—or No-thing.
A man who attains this state might well describe a void—
an abyss in which the ego dies. From this we get many misunderstood commentaries about the annihilation of the self.
Perhaps the nearest parallel in ordinary life is of love, when
the lover totally forgets himself in the beloved, only in this
case the 'dark mistress' Shakespeare speaks of in the sonnets
does not sue for breach of promise once the affair is over.
This love is of a cosmic order, the first step in the courtship
between the heavenly bridegroom of Kether and his bride in
earthly Malcut. Daat is the veil, beyond which lies knowledge and being of the Objective Universe.

Netzah—Eternity or the repeating Sephira, is in man all
the involuntary processes including the autonomic system.
It is the first Sephira to actually be seen at work in the
physical realm. Netzah at the root of the active column of
the Tree provides the force for all the vital functions, ranging from the heartbeat to the digestive processes of the gut.
This Sephira not only manifests in all the inward cyclic processes but in the outward too—the instinct of attraction
and repulsion between the sexes, the ebb and flow of desires.
Here is Nature at work, creative, for ever building up then
dissolving, circling a myriad tiny daily changes that are
linked with the motions of the external year. In Netzah
resides love but of a different order from that of Hesed above.
This instinctive love emerges each spring when thousands
upon thousands of young men suddenly become attached
to young women, each one of course a unique relationship

to those concerned. This phenomenon has been observed over many centuries with delight, the mature realising it is part of a cycle, an eternally repeating Spring festival in the body of mankind.

Netzah in the human organism is the provider of the instinctive powerhouse. It maintains not only the body's health but provides energy for Hod, the voluntary processes, the counterbalance on the receptive side of the Tree. Hod, as we have said, may be translated from the Hebrew as 'Splendour', but its root also lies in the word 'reverberation'—the Cabalists we are told had a traditional technique of putting off casual inquirers by deliberately misleading. The root word of Hod applies very precisely to the voluntary processes. This includes all the senses which can be directed and respond or reverberate to incoming data. Beside the obvious five receptors man is not only sensitive to heat, smell, sound and all other physical impressions, he is also open to the meaning contained within the sound of words, music, the marks seen as mathematics, symbols and forms. A man may receive physical, emotional and intellectual stimuli; all of which need to be communicated to the interior world of the organism. Thus a remarkable abstract concept, or the sight of a naked girl, may have great impact on a man and yet not be received by the same Sephiroth within him. The excitement generated in these two cases could be Hod and Netzah respectively, though not necessarily in other situations.

Beside responding to the outer world, as does the whole of the passive column of which Hod is the bottom rung, this Sephira also checks Netzah. A man may find a certain girl unbearably attractive but Hod controls his desire. This is the Sephira of mental input or education as well. Good conventional manners are assimilated here as are all acquired skills, which are then stored in the brain to become conditioned memories and reflexes, be they general know-

ledge or physical responses. A soldier's training in arms
may be second nature in battle but it still belongs to Hod,
though his desire to survive is Netzah.

These two lowest Sephiroth provide the manifestation of
the active and passive principles in the physical realm which
begins at this point on the Tree. The Netzah-Hod level and
below is what we normally see of the World. Observe a rush-
hour scene in a big city; everyone's eyes are blank, far away
in dreams, as their Hod-Netzah systems guide them without
fail along routine paths. In work and leisure Hod and Netzah
carry out endless tasks, operating machines, reading, writing,
running a home, bringing up children, socialising, playing
physical or intellectual games and making love. Between and
below these two lowest of the Functional Sephiroth lies the
Universe of our mundane perception. Yesod is the mind
pivot of the world of materiality and action. Ego consciousness on the middle pillar its English name 'Foundation'
indicates its importance in perceiving the Universe about
us.

Yesod in man relates to that strange part of him wherein
he forms images. On the central column but on a lower scale
than Tepheret, it is like a screen-mirror continually reflecting and projecting into the ordinary consciousness what is
presented by the paths flowing into it. These paths suspend
it amid the four points of Tepheret, Netzah, Hod and Malcut
and through it a man sees the inner and outer worlds. Yesod
is supplied by data coming from Hod, energy from Netzah
and the physical vehicle to live in by Malcut. Ideally it is
the servant of Tepheret the Essential Nature which is in turn
but the steward of a man, for whom Kether the Crown is
King. However, as so often happens a man forgets quite early
in childhood the lucid observer of his Essential Nature and
begins only to trust Yesod, the ever accumulating ego Persona
which his world and those about him wish him to acquire.
If he comes from one strata of society it will take on this

form, if from another, that. Moreover his family will require that he behaves this way, his school friends that. These and other habits and attitudes are assimulated in his Yesod and form his picture of himself, an artefact ego. While Hod supplies the material in his response to the external world and Netzah to the inner, his imitation and comparisons of what he perceives will build up a picture of his relationship to life about him. His attractions and repulsions create yet another form, all of which are lodged in the psychological Yesodic armour which is slowly accreting over his Essential Nature, partly to protect it and partly to imprison. This is the Persona, Latin for mask, a quite accurate description for what is called personality. Here is what the world sees, and sometime with a man who has lost touch with himself, what he himself thinks is his true nature. A face may be bland and the manner charming but to the discerning eye this may be a man imprisoned in a psychological iron mask.

Yesod is in its correct position a superb minister. It gathers in all the information from the physical and psychological realms and focuses it into readable images. Thus you remember scenes with sounds and smells, recall telephone numbers, set out the elements of a problem to be solved, replay or rehearse a situation that has been or is to be enacted. It is a reflector of what cannot be seen directly of the psyche or body. It is a personal mental read-out screen for a working scientist, and the inner projection room for an artist. Yesod hovers, a fragile ephemeral structure held in equilibrium on the lowest rung of consciousness. In sleep it runs a midnight newsreel movie of the day and the current problems, often using actors and settings supplied by other Sephiroth. In the case of madness, Yesod appears to be the real world because the connection with Malcut below is blocked or severed. On death Yesod is said to rewind the film of a man's life before him. Though not proven it is an interesting speculation.

Yesod then is a fixed mask outwards and a chameleon mirror inwards, the mask's configuration distorting or clarifying the picture presented to the inner consciousness. Here is held a man's body image, the awareness of just how long his arms are, the knowledge of how much he can raise his voice to get a desired effect. This is a linking reference arena for all he has learnt, so that if he is a savage or a sophisticate he can at least recognise the physical or intellectul clothes he wears. However, like the Emperor's new suit, it is not always as substantial as he would like to believe, for though it appears solid, it is but a useful mirage borrowed for a lifetime to deal with familiar contexts, and when confronted with an important decision out of its field of reference it is quite inadequate. Observe yourself when two friends from totally different spheres meet you off your home ground, a mild schizophrenia occurs—this is the Persona—or one or two aspects of it, whereas a man in touch with his Essential Nature is the same to everyone. Yesod can be a bridge or a barrier. It can be the vehicle of creative imagination or a retreat for illusion. It is the principal eye we have of ourselves and the world. Dependent on the dullness or translucence of the screen-mirror, the active or passive state of our mask, we are on the bottom rung of consciousness. The choice is to wake up or remain half asleep.

The second and just as important feature of Yesod, the Foundation, in its relation to man, is its correspondence to the sexual act. This Sephira situated on the main axis of the Tree receives energy directly via Tepheret from Daat and Kether. Focused in Yesod with the inflowing from the male and female sides of the Tree, it makes the sexual triad. This is because the active-passive forces are brought into creative relationship by the pillar of equilibrium. True, the three pairs of outer Sephiroth are higher on the Tree, but they are primarily functional opposites. Only the central Sephiroth can take on the unique role of transformation.

Yesod can trigger conception in sexual union, and it is also the conscious basis or foundation of spiritual birth. Tepheret is concerned with the discovery of the Self, while Daat is the point where that identity vanishes in the void of Cosmic consciousness before union with Kether.

In outer life Yesod is the great driving force. Sex is more than just the act, it generates more than children. Commerce and the arts know that men love women and women adore men. Advertising, films, plays, restaurants, clothes, a myriad activities are devoted to this mutual dynamic that gives the drama of life its spice. The machine age will never replace the interaction between the sexes and the vast amount of time and energy spent on it. The driving force of Yesod is found in politics as well as the dance hall. Men strive to prove themselves by getting to the top of the heap and even the highly technical operation of reaching the moon has a strong dream and phallic—Yesodic—quality.

This powerhouse is vital to life. Without it a man has no strength to draw upon. Energy may flow down from above, but here is a choice of direction. Through the conversion of this abundant force a man may take a step up the ladder of self-realisation, begin his return. He will, if he does, move in opposition to the descending octave of Creation and retrace the path back to Creation's source. Perhaps this is why this Sephira is called Foundation.

Malcut in man is his physical body. The English translation —Kingdom, refers to the terrestrial elements. The body is composed literally of earth, all the bones, tissues and cells constructed of mineral and traces of metal; enough iron for a fair-sized nail, we were told at school. These earth elements form for the most part the structure of the body, and are held in position like a standing wave, in as much as they sustain the body's form and systems while continually changing its substance.

The principle embodied in the water element also continually passes through the organic standing wave known as the body. In blood and all the body fluids water circulates every zone passing not only along the finest-gauge capillaries but through cell walls. Without the element water the body would shrivel up, cease the vital exchanges found in metabolism. These internal tides not only maintain the easy flow of the material passing into and out of the body but help in the process of growth.

Air, the third elemental state, is manifest as a major contributor to the energy-generating cycle of the body, but it is also to be seen as the various gases present. These may permeate blood and tissue, and deprivation of one gaseous element may cause a serious imbalance, even death. Man prior to birth is an aquatic creature, living in the fluids of the womb. On birth organic doors close and open and with the first breath comes a distinct quantum jump into mammal life, even if no other development follows. In the air, besides the well known gases are several others, some very rare and difficult to trace. It is said that in an awakened spiritual state the body can extract these fine elements, precipitating yet another birth, but this time of consciousness.

Fire, the lightest element, is a symbol for radiant energy, flame emitting heat, light and many other frequencies. In man this might be seen as that property which permeates the whole organism and which is so obviously absent in a corpse. It might, in one state, be heat, or in another the Bio-electrical envelope which surrounds the living. It could be thought, or psychological illumination, or even in animals as primitive spirit. It is however discernible as the subtlest materiality present in the physical body. The electrical fields within living cells might only be the crudest description of a vibratory process emanating from the DNA molecules composing and governing them. These molecules in turn may only be the printed circuits for receiving that curious influx of energy known as Life, for it is apparent that when any organism is cut off from Nature or the vital radiance of the Sun it droops from lack of stimulating input, and with complete deprivation of whatever fire on earth is, it dies.

For Man, Malcut is also the physical Universe. When he looks out through a telescope or down a microscope he sees Malcut, the densest level of Materiality. Even his radio telescopes only register Malcut—the physical radiant fields surrounding elemental bodies. The fine pictures of the galaxy Andromeda are but the photographs of a quite solid body in a defused state. And electron microscope pictures of atomic structures merely film their physical appearance, though we might guess at why they form those latticed patterns. The next realm, that of the Universe of Formation, lies out of physical sight closer to the vision seen in an artist's studio than in a scientific laboratory.

Malcut is the world we are most familiar with, for men tend to see results rather than causes. Preferring the end product as it is now fixed, we often forget the actions that created it. The Rembrandts scattered about the art galleries of the world are the residue of his creative process, the dim physical sketch of what he really saw. In Malcut however is all that went before, it contains every quality of all the Sephiroth concentrated into matter. The whole of natural evolution is present in a man's body. Every organic stage from conception has to be passed through before human birth. With maturity, when Nature has completed her job of outfitting, the next evolutionary process, of consciousness, is taken on by a man himself.

The Cabalists have a saying: 'In Kether is Malcut, and Malcut is in Kether.' This can be taken many ways, but in this case it is like the analogue of a seed. Within the tough dense kernel of a chestnut resides not just one possible new tree, but a whole forest of generations. Another meaning is that within the thickest of matters is spirit; imprisoned, yes, but present and always ready for the reascent back to the Absolute. This is Malcut, the lowest of the Sephiroth yet the most loaded with potential. In man, within the vehicle of his physical body, is the possibility of rapid development. In the difficult situation of life on Earth maximum resistance creates great potential and therefore possibilities. This is backed by all the resources locked up within man. A delicate, but tough mechanism, the body, soul and spirit, is a fantastic powerhouse full of many different kinds of fuel, each with a particular function and quality. The million parts and sophisticated systems of the first rocket to the Moon were crude compared to just the machine part of a man and he is designed to go higher, even beyond the Sun.

Looking back at the Tree of Life in terms of man, we see it as a living organism, each Sephira balancing its complement and contributing to a whole integrated system. By study of ourselves we may recognise the various parts and even observe occasionally from which Sephira we began a thought, a feeling or an action. This will be studied later in detail as we become more familiar with the cosmogram. One final word. The Tree, when superimposed on a man, reveals that we only see a fraction of his nature. Besides his body and personality, the rest of him is invisible to the physical world. With the aid of the Tree of Life we may come to perceive his soul. Time allows us a glimpse of him; but the babe, the child, and adolescent he was, are gone; and what he might be has not yet come. The Tree is the only permanent feature in a man, in that he is modelled on an eternal universal design. This is the full man, containing all Creation, and in the image of He who made him.

VI

Tree and Gods

Having related the Sephiroth to man, we now apply the ancient maxim 'As above so below' to demonstrate the Tree of Life on another dimension. Taking the Sky as a larger World and using the argument that what was loosely called the macrocosm is modelled on the same universal plan, Cabalists formulated the Tree in terms of the Greco-Roman Gods and their corresponding planets. This enabled the Tree to be viewed in wider vision using the myths about the Gods to describe the Sephiroth. In addition to this the solar system was arranged as an organism, but seen from the position of earth which is centred appropriately in Malcut the lowest Sephira. This fitted into the Ptolemaic world picture, which contrary to modern scientific belief was not a naïve picture of the solar system but a relative framework (the only basic one we have in a vast universe) as seen from man's situation. This geocentric scheme, combined with the Tree, was one of the earliest theories of relativity, taking into account not only the physical positions of the heavenly bodies, but also their functional relationship within the solar system.

Beginning this time with Malcut we start with Mother Earth, or in Cabalistic terms the Bride. Situated at the bottom of the Tree it is the realm of the elements; in concrete physics, it is a rocky ball of minerals and metals covered with a skin of water, surrounded by an atmosphere of air and clothed far out into space by the electro-magneto-sphere.

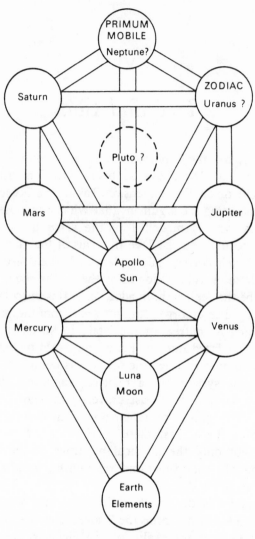

Gods and planets

This layered coat of radiation is the fire element of the Earth. Together these various states of matter, solid, liquid, gas and radiation, form the body of the planet. Deep inside it, on, or near the hard surface, is a thin living film called Nature, which contains not only the flora and fauna of Pan, but this strange creature called man, the most sensitive organism of natural evolution.

Malcut is our physical environment. Embedded in it we lose sight of it. As our bodies are composed of it, we forget it is a temporary form through which the four elemental states pass. At death the physical mould is broken and the elements disperse, each to its level in the planet. Malcut is the Bride, the great Terrestrial Mother recognised by all civilisations, be they agricultural or industrial. Gaea, the Greek Earth Mother, was the great provider and nourisher. Without her, men, animals and plants could not live, and she must be wooed and husbanded for raw material and food. Female by nature, this Sephira adapts and adopts the character of the influences converging upon it, yet passive and immobile as it might appear this maternal, elemental kingdom is the womb of spirit being reborn. Malcut is what science might call physics, and though crude in relation to metaphysics it is the elemental end of a vast cosmic spectrum. In Greek mythology out of Gaea the Great Earth Mother was born Uranus, the starry sky, and out of their union came the Giant Titans, one of whom was Chronos, known to us in Latin as Saturn—the God of Time.

About the Earth, its satellite Luna, the moon, orbits. Enclosed within the planet's gravitational and magnetic field the moon's pull in counter balance, not only drags the Earth's seas up and down, but draws all the fluids within every living thing, so that Nature responds in a daily and monthly rhythm of ebb and flow. Plants grow in monthly pulses as they expand and contract their spreads, the moisture content of their sap waxing and waning in their tissue.

Animals on land and in the sea are affected by these lunar fluctuations, their hunting and breeding habits coinciding with the Moon's phases.

Men too are influenced; the cycles of crime in big city police records showing a monthly rise and fall. Blood coagulates faster at certain lunar times and anyone who has worked in an asylum will know the distinct restlessness that occurs at full moon.

Fable has it that Selene, Goddess of the Moon, though ruler of the realm of Pan, loved Endymion the shepherd who represented mankind. However, she could only love him through his sleep, reach him through his dreams—or the Sephira of Yesod. Here also lies the pendulum of Nature's mechanism; in humanity the regulation of mass cycles, and in the individual, personal moods.

In Diana the huntress and Artemis the multi-breasted goddess, the Moon's birth-death aspects are shown, each deity describing respectively the new and full nodal points in the lunar appearance. This constantly altering shape and size is created by the Moon's motion along the Zodiac, as she progresses through her daily rising and settings. Besides these motions, she wanders back and forth across the celestial equator and occasionally looms nearer to earth, thus completing the impression of an endless variation, a constant mutation within a system of revolutions. From a Cabalistic viewpoint we see the principle of eternal change; the Moon's position in relation to the Earth and Sun continually altering the mask of reflection. In man's psyche we see the same thing—the Yesodic screen-image seen is never the same, yet it repeats endlessly in variation. Under certain conditions the Moon is evocative of romance and all the fascination that love song and story tell, but daylight and down to earth facts break the illusion, when the reality of a child's conception and its subsequent complications dawn. The lunatic, aptly named, lives exclusively within this realm of

imagination, the Sephira of Yesod. In his case he is discon-
nected from Malcut, the World outside.

Yesod, here represented by the Moon, is also sex, and
governs, it is said, the female menstrual cycle. Another
aspect—Witchcraft, the applied use of the Yesodic energy
and imagine-making—is symbolised in Hecate, the lunar goddess of enchantments.

There are many facets to Yesod on this scale. For the Earth
on this dimension Time is different. If we take one year or a
complete round of the seasons as one breath measure for
our planet, the moon's orbit would appear as a whizzing
stone weaving a latticed shell of rock, light, and pull about
the Earth.

Compared with the rest of the solar system the Earth and
her large moon are twins—in effect a single organisation, or
one being. To the other planets, the Earth might appear to
wear a lunar face (rather like a thicker version of Saturn's
rings would seem to us), though to the Earth itself it would
be but a see-through veil. Indeed a celestial twin, the moon,
nearest body to the Earth, is so close it acts like a reflective
screen between us and outer space. Through this shimmer-
ing whirling mask every influence going out or coming in
must pass. It is in the same position as the Persona is to a
man, lying correspondingly between the Sun of his Essential
Nature and the Earth of his body. Bridge and barrier, the
moon both joins and separates, its pale screen reflecting what
the Earth cannot directly look upon. In Cabalistic terms
Yesod—the moon—lies on the axis of consciousness, but it is
also at the lower meeting point, on the Tree, of the inflow
from the combined active and passive influence of the
planets.

Mercury, in the Sephira Hod, is the Messenger to the Gods.
He stands in astronomical terms nearest to Apollo the Sun.
Through his orbit the solar rays must pass before reaching
any of the other planets. His is the sphere of transmission,

having no potent force of his own because of his minute size. Mercury was also considered to take on and enhance the qualities of the other planets he came into conjunction with. His talent lay, it was said, in his flexibility—his mercurial nature—which enabled him to adapt, modify, use and throw away whatever came into his field. He was the God of thieves and merchants, the rapid sleight of hand, and of exchange and trade. He was the deity concerned with the acquisition of knowledge and its dispensation. Witty, cunning, deft, fleet of foot, all his qualities are of the essence of Hod—Reverberation or Splendour. As in the voluntary processes in man with their many senses, Mercury represents the versatile intelligence that scans for data, picks it up, passes it on, then scans again. Consider the ability and mechanism of the human eye and ear. In themselves they are always in movement reverberating and transmitting information. With the Gods, Mercury performed the same function, keeping them informed and informing in a continuous round of errands, while amusing himself with endless games and love affairs. Of these the three most important were Persephone, an aspect of Mother Earth—Malcut, Hecate, moon goddess of witchcraft and childbirth—Yesod, and Aphrodite, Venus, the goddess of Nature—Netzah. All these compose the bottom triad of the Tree of Life with Mercury acting as the outer sensor or intelligence.

Mercury, besides being the Divine Herald, was also the receptacle of ordinary and extraordinary knowledge. Because of his ability to fly anywhere at great speed he knew about everything. This included geography, history, science, all the matters relating to study—the realm of Hod. Moreover, because he carried the caduceus, the rod entwined with two snakes, the symbol of his office, he had access to the knowledge about—I repeat—'about' metaphysics. The caduceus is another version of the Tree of Life. The rod is the pillar of equilibrium and each snake describes the active and passive principles passing down from the winged head of the rod to its foot. However, this is a book to be read and studied as an introduction, as are all of the treatises on the Hermetic (Hermes or Mercurial) sciences. Here is the theoretical field, the point of input necessary before practice. Mercury had many skills ranging from handicrafts to the manipulation of ideas—all acquired. He was also a great liar and deceiver, and in man one knows how the senses can also mislead, when, for instance, a mercurial problem like an optical illusion is presented. Perhaps for this reason Mercury and the Sephira of Hod is the God and province of magicians, scientists and charlatans.

Astronomically Mercury is only rarely seen, for its motion is swift and too close to the Sun. Yet without its presence just outside the Sun's corona who knows what the inner balance of the solar system might be? As in the mechanics of a watch, a hair spring, though light and fine, nevertheless governs, by its critical position and function, the delicate regulation of the whole mechanism. In man's body is the same thing, one extra grain of this or that substance may mean the difference between madness or sanity and the Sephira Hod keeps this balance in conjunction with Netzah.

Netzah is Venus in this view of the Tree of Life. Venus is the goddess of beauty, love and instinct. She is depicted as a naked woman, lovely in form. In her is embodied the power to stir desire. She is the goddess of Nature, spring and growth. Her power to arouse is partly centred in her grace—her preoccupation is with beauty, perhaps because of her marriage to the ugliest god on Olympus, Vulcan. The stories of her amorous affairs are endless, one continuous cycle of attraction and rejection. This could be a key to the Cabalistic designation 'Eternity'. Another could be the ever returning Spring which is her special domain. Here everything is renewed after the nadir of Winter. This is the vital impulse in the endless chain necessary to maintain Nature. Without courtship there would be no marriage, without the union no children to repeat the cycle of generation. Spring is the period of beauty, the Earth clothes herself with blossom and the creatures sing and dance in a great game of love. Man is subject to this vital impulse and many of his arts are devoted to the subject. Venus is the planet and goddess of the Sephira Netzah, her morning and evening star appearance marking the systole and diastole of a gentle cycle that is eternally pulsing through Nature and the solar system. In man she represents the involuntary processes, such as the gut and heart. But Netzah also defines that which we find attractive, and then repulsive. Venus's love adventures have this quality of seduction then rejection. There is never the stable consummation of a situation. Her being was concerned with ease, the effortless. Drudgery and strain were not in her experience. The heart pumps without thought and the stomach digests with no prompting, and when either of these is troubled the organism is, as the very word explains—diseased.

Charm and grace are the attributes of Venus. From her the arts of music and painting come, as does poetry. Netzah is to the arts what Hod is to the sciences. However, while Hod observes, as the receptive side of the Tree, Netzah is on the creative, and this is why though science in the twentieth century is dominant, it cannot entirely reject the power of the arts, which indicate the driving force in a community. The world's great books, pictures and music reveal more potently the mood of a given time than any machine or new discovery.

Venus is the counterbalance to Mercury and vice versa. It is the desire for a more pleasant standard of living that encourages science. Venus, or the power of love, it is said, makes the world go round. This cliché is more true than imagined. Without Netzah a man would not want to work. either for a new car, a fine house or a beautiful wife. This force is quite different from Yesodic energy. It is biological, natural, rooted in the need to give and receive, the reciprocal arrangement observed in the cell, man and Nature as a whole. Venus always seeks that which is desirable, away from the painful, whether it is hunger or what is uncomfortable, or towards the pleasant, be it a new love or a familiar pleasure in an eternal graceful roundabout.

The position of Tepheret in this cosmic scheme is occupied by the Sun. Tepheret in man is defined as the Essential Nature or the individual self. This is Apollo in the central position of a man and the soler system. Nearly all paths lead to the Sun, feeding energy in, before they are radiated out again. In man this same Sephira could be called the Watcher, in that it perceives directly in to all the Sephiroth except Malcut. Apollo was known as the God of Truth to the Greeks, moreover he was renowned for his outstanding awesome Beauty—which is the English translation for Tepheret. His oracle at Delphi was famous for its penetrating answers, very apt for the God of Light.

Tepheret is the Sun, almost impossible to look directly upon. Such was the face of Apollo that a glance at it by the unprepared might blind them for life. Seen from the view of a man this might well correspond to seeing more than a man could bear to know about himself; this is why most men live in Yesod—the moon of themselves—preferring to see only by reflection the light of their real nature.

Astronomically the Sun lies at the centre of the solar system. It is the pivot around which all the other planets turn. Modern scientists tell us not only does it radiate heat, light and a large range of radiation and particles, but it also absorbs, sucks in vast quantities of inter-stellar gas as it moves round the Milky Way. This could be seen as positive energy and negative matter coming in from the left and right columns of the Tree to feed the being embodied in the astronomical and psychological Sun.

The Sun not only illuminates all the planets but also shines light on the smallest particles the human eye can detect, so fine is its wave-lengths. Psychologically the same phenomenon occurs within a man who is in touch with his own being as focused in Tepheret. This *is* him. True, only a miniature being compared to Kether, as our Sun is to the Galaxy, but it is nevertheless his own individuality. This is Apollo, the God who could only speak the truth, whose silver bow could strike at any distance and yet whose golden lyre could delight the other Gods. Apollo has an awesome aspect. In him is brilliance, the quality so often ascribed to great men. Enlightenment is a term not used idly or just for poetic reasons. It is a precise description of the nature of Tepheret, for it is the Sun of a man, the point exactly between Heaven and Earth, Kether and Malcut, in him. Here spirit is half caught in form. It partakes of the upper and lower parts of the Tree, except where it is guarded from burning up the Earth by Yesod, and from losing its temporary individuality by the invisible gate of Daat.

Apollo was considered as a direct link between the Gods and men. His position on the Tree of Life and in the solar system backs up this assertion. Through the Sun God, all the Sephiroth can be reached. In a man centred on his inner Essential Nature every part of his being may be known. Here is the Delphic Oracle in a person. Ask it a real question and it will reply—the simple Truth. This is the voice that speaks occasionally from our own inner depths of space. This is the interior Sun—the Apollo most of the time we dare not face for fear of his penetrating glance. Mercury, the myth says, stole from Apollo; but by divination, that is, by direct perception, the thief was found out. How may be cunning, Netzah distracting with her pleasures as Yesod is with her dreams, but ultimately Tepheret blasts through, if only at the moment before death.

Tepheret—Apollo—the Sun lies on the axis of consciousness. Through it passes the majority of forces flowing down the Tree and through the solar system. Behind it lies the Sun of the sun—Kether, the Crown through which stream the Divine emanations.

Gevura is symbolised in Mars, the traditional god and planet of war. These symbols, it would appear, were designed with great care by the ancient world, certainly with as much attention as a modern computer or aero engine. If we examine each symbol and its component parts we will see they were not constructed by a vague superstitious collection of Greek witch doctors, but were the product of highly sophisticated thinking, each image a whole book in its own right. The chief difference between the ancient and modern way of looking at the Universe is scale and language. While we know much about size, great and small, they understood depth and dimension. This is seen very clearly in twentieth-century metaphysics and its confusion.

In the symbol of Mars are many ideas. Superficially he seems only to mean strife, but a closer look reveals that it always takes two to quarrel. Contention cannot be on its own. This points to the dual aspect of the God, and the Aye and Nay, the for and against, the pro and con. This is the essential quality of Gevura. At this point on the Tree decisions are continually being made, comparisons set up and selections carried out. In its most dramatic form a battlefield is the deciding ground, one side or the other conquering. In man, his day-to-day emotional faculty is continually assessing, be it like or dislike of people, ideas or things. Its hallmark is a clear-cut judgement. This is Gevura or the sword of Mars, dividing this from that with one quick cut, while his shield parries and balances. This is the passive aspect of his nature.

Mars is sometimes known as ruthless, but he also has been known to run from the field of battle howling, like a coward. This was usually when he was confronted by Pallas Athene,

the war goddess whose coolness, courage and intelligence
always got the better of Mars, for when roused he tended to
fly into a rage which reduced his accuracy of judgement,
vital in battle. Here we have some interesting parallels in
man's psyche.

Mars also has a special relationship with Venus. Married
to the ugly Vulcan, she set up an adulterous relationship
with the war god. This combination was delightful for a
time, but it caused Mars humiliation before his fellow gods
when Vulcan by means of a fine almost invisible net tied the
undiscerning lovers up for an Olympian exposé. This was
a lesson for Mars, his sharp eye, swift action had been
softened and dulled by Venus. Netzah had swamped Gevura.
Passion had blunted judgement and this temptation has sent
more than just illicit lovers to the wall.

Mars's armour is very interesting. The function of these
plates of metal and leather is to prevent hurt, to limit injury
and protect the body. It does, however, constrict the wearer,
set a clear boundary between the hard exterior and soft inner
body. It is said by Cabalists that Gevura not only makes
severe judgements if not balanced by merciful Hesed, but
over-confines the potent energy coming from the positive
side of the Tree. Here the symbol of Mars acts like a control, as a para-military force does within a community under
the law—Binah. Mars is at its best a good police force, at its
worst the Gestapo. In the human organism he represents all
those processes that separate out the various substances and
energies to where they are needed.

Mars is by its very name Martial, force under discipline,
precise orders carried out without question, but it can only
operate well under the restraint of something higher. The
intelligent soldier hardly ever needs to use violence, though
his actions must be decisive.

Of the planet Mars we know little except its apparent
movements are sudden and occasionally erratic, sometimes

drawing remarkably close to the Earth, at others pulling right away, his red face is just detected as an unflickering point. This is very much like day to day emotion, and while one should not parallel the analogue too closely it is interesting, that next to Venus or Netzah, Mars is the closest planet to the Earth.

Jupiter occupies the position of Hesed on the Tree of Life. This is the point of expansion, of great energy before it is checked by Gevura. Also attributed to this Sephira are the qualities of magnificence, magnanimity, mercy, all marks of Jupiter the beneficent god—though when uncontrolled, a danger with his endless largesse. This is shown very clearly in the round of myths connected with his loves. In these he pursues mortal women and goddesses to spread his vast reservoir of most potent seed, leading to numerous half-immortals and heroes. This is the particular power of Hesed. One story well illustrates the effect of undiluted magnificence. Semele, daughter of King Cadmus, asked to see her god-lover in all his glory. Jupiter attempted to dissuade her but in the end he gave in and she was blasted out of existence by his spendour like a snowflake in a furnace.

Jupiter was King on Olympus, about him circled the other gods. From the point of view of the solar system this could be taken several ways. Whereas the Sun appears to be the pivot of the planetary organisation it may be in fact only a terminal pole, with the planet Pluto at the outer end. Moreover, Jupiter not only lies roughly in the centre of the planetary chain stretching out from the Sun but it is the largest planet. This is more than significant, because the size of Jupiter is the greatest a molecular body can be before the spontaneous generation of an atomic process can begin. The Sun is running down, whereas there is reason to believe Jupiter is growing. It already emits radio frequencies close to the Sun's. In addition to this, the king-sized planet has a full retinue of twelve satellites, some larger than our

Moon. It is already a miniature solar system, though this is mere interesting speculation.

As a God, Jupiter generated many minor cults as well as children. Dionysus, one of his sons, was not only known for his exuberant festivals of wine, but for madness. Yet another example of excess use of bountiful power.

The position of Hesed on the Tree might well explain the negative aspect of Jupiter. Receiving the Lightning Flash of divine energy from Binah, Jupiter also sits immediately below Hochma and takes in the pure vertical input of masculine energy from above. This Sephira, be it planet or person, if blocked will be charged with such a dynamic that there must be a release or explosion—hence Jupiter's profligacy—or in human terms genius, and productivity. Van Gogh the painter is a good example. Driven by the unbalanced positive energy from Hochma and Hesed he had to paint or go mad, which he eventually did when he found it impossible to control the force passing through him. Dostoyevski the writer as an epileptic had the same problem with his frenetic and prolific vision. Jupiter may seem at first sight all beneficent, but the god was not always a pleasant despot. He carried a thunderbolt which he threw at unwary mortals and his aim was not always accurate. This wide-angled spray is characteristic of both Jupiter and Gedulah, or Greatness, another Hebrew name for Hesed. While dynamic proliferation, creation and magnanimity are needed, they must be disciplined—by Gevura. Perhaps this is why Jupiter could never really master his wife Hera for all his power.

Moving back up the Tree along the Lightning Flash we pass through the invisible Sephira known as Daat—Knowledge—before we reach Binah, or Saturn in this planetary scheme. Some modern Cabalists not only describe this transition point as the entry into what is known as the supernal triad of Kether, Hochma and Binah, but ascribe this position to the recently discovered planet Pluto. Now while any thoughts on this idea may be at present hypothetical, they are very useful as a way of considering this intermediary Sephira.

The God Pluto was the brother of both Neptune and Jupiter. He was King of the underworld, or to put it in Christian terms the Outer Darkness—in an astronomical sense roughly Pluto's remote position in the solar system. Moreover he had a famous cap of invisibility. This could be read in two ways: that he was monarch of the dead, of those who have passed out of our dimension of sight; or that his processes are so slow (the planet has the orbital period of 247 years) that one lifetime is not enough to observe its full cycle. Pluto is the King of death, the planet of the most profound transformation man can physically witness. This event comes and goes, nothing can prevent it; suddenly a being who has been a piece of human furniture in a society or family has vanished, disappeared into another world, the realm of shades. Hades' Gate may indeed be knowledge; for it is said that on death, everything learnt is reviewed as the past life is rapidly uncoiled in an ecstatic flash, of every pleasure, pain, ignorance and understanding lived. Here at the invisible door the experience and essence of a man is further distilled, the limiting ego evaporated for ever in the void of the divine Father and Mother before the final union with the Creator.

Pluto orbits at the very edge of the solar system. Beyond lies the realm of the local star cluster and, containing this, the vast galactic arm of the Milky Way. Pluto's strange eccentric orbit is the margin and frontier of the planetary world, and who knows what barrier or bridge this dark unseen planet describes?

The god Pluto was much feared on the surface of the earth; but it must be remembered that his wife Persephone, a daughter of earth, comes to the surface from the underworld as Spring each year.

Pluto is certainly an unknown both as a planet and a Cabalistic principle, but this we do know, that Daat is a point of profound transformation whether you are travelling up or down the Tree of Life.

The Sephira of Binah is filled by the god and planet Saturn. According to myth tradition Saturn or Chronos (the Greek name) was one of the elder gods or titans, Jupiter being his son, who later displaced him as King. This appears to indicate a clear differentiation between the upper triad of Binah, Hochma, and Kether; and the middle triad of Hesed, Gevura, and Tepheret. Saturn the god of form is in the correct position on the Tree; for it is the first passive principle, the cosmic Mother who changes the energy of Hochma into formulation. It is said that Saturn is the original Old Father Time. Time is the first limitation, out of it unfolds change, and change means the interrelationship of energy and form. Saturn is also associated with those things that are old and proven. It is the conservative element at its worst, and the perception of eternal principles at its best. In man Binah represents understanding; that is, the recognition of what is. This realisation takes perhaps three quarters of a life span. Old age is called the period of Saturn. Positively viewed, this phase is the era of contemplation at the closing of the circle of life. Repeating patterns are seen; the interweaving of events, the workings of fate, and the ebb and flow of the forces of life and death. These things can only be revealed from a great distance, height or depth. Saturn is reputed to have just that viewpoint. He is perhaps the most philosophical of the gods, having experienced it all many times in his position as father of the King of Olympia. To him, in his orbit far outside Jupiter and the inner planets, all events are encompassed by his slower year. He has seen it all before.

Cast in the form of an old man, lean and bearded with a scythe, he is often associated with grimness and melancholy. This more commonplace image overlays an intelligent gravity, a mind that sees an overall plan. In this long vision Saturn is supreme. He can set out an idea, create a master design, knowing its results well beyond the time horizon of the other gods. From Binah or Saturn flows not only the received and passed on divine impulse, but a form, a set of principles, by which the Lightning Flash may manifest itself in the lower worlds. This in architectural terms would be the layout of a new town. Buildings may come and go, but the type of development, urban, market, or manufacturing, will remain the same for a long time before it changes its basic scheme. This is Saturn, god of conservation as well as form.

Binah is sometimes known as the Mother because its passive role is embodied in Saturn. Saturn is resistant to change. The other planets rapidly alter their position relative to the Sun, but he plods on, carrying his rings of limitation with him. These rings may be the product of an event occurring before organic life on Earth, they certainly indicate a major change of balance within the solar system, and this is mentioned in many world myths on the origin of the Universe. From the point of view of man, Saturn is the furthest planet that can be seen by the normal naked eye. Here for ordinary man the solar system finishes. Telescopes may bring the image of the planet nearer, but nothing else. This was to the ancients, the limit, beyond which little else was known or perceived, except by speculation and illumination. At Binah this would appear to be correct; for Hochma is almost as undefinable as Kether, whereas Binah at least has the first recognisable impressions of an outline. This is the essence of Saturn; the inception of Chronos—time and form.

The Sephira of Hochma is traditionally filled by the Zodiac. This is the band round the sky centred on the path of the Sun. Besides enclosing the orbits of all the other planets, the Zodiac defines twelve phases of a continuous cosmic process. The idea is ancient and is embodied, on the level of man, in the twelve tribes of Israel and the disciples of Christ. In this number all the human types were expressed, thus forming the complete circle of Mankind. In the realm of Nature, a similar process may be seen in the twelve phases of the natural year. To take an example. The Sun when in the sign of Taurus is manifest in the northern hemisphere of Earth as Spring, the time of courtship, mating, nest-building, growth, and birth. Precisely opposite in the natural year lies Scorpio, the sign the Sun passes through in Autumn. Here we witness the falling of the leaves and drying out of cast-off fruit. The fields are brown and the summer birds have already flown. It is a time of decay, the beginning of the end of the natural cycle when the vital energies of Life are spent. Everywhere there is the smell of rot and death —and yet within each fallen fruit lies a new seed, at the root of every shrivelled leaf is a new bud. Taurus and Scorpio are cosmic opposites: one the entry into physical life and the other the departure from it in physical death. Yet each contains at its heart the inner content of the other, both are a mirror in Nature of archetype law—in this lies the essence of Hochma.

The Zodiac in Hochma contains all possibilities. The potential streaming out from this Sephira is enormous. Before it is received and contained by Binah any combination is possible. The Zodiac describes twelve broad definitions, but each one of these is full of variation in its own right. The potentiality summed up in the sign of Capricorn is vast. Here is stability and strength, order, hierarchy, patience, and time. In Aries we have the dynamic of initiative, originality, courage, skill, sacrifice, and vision; and these are mere human manifestations of these root principles! Multiplied by twelve, plus the several levels these archetypes operate at, we have the full range from which a particular Tree of Life may develop, be it a man or the twelve Olympians.

At this point we may see how the emanations streaming out from Kether are changed, by passing through each Sephira, until they reach their final form in Malcut. From the conversion into actual potential by the action of Hochma, the emanations are formulated into major principles by Binah, these are developed and expanded within their context by Hesed, then refined by the discrimination of Gevura into the recognisable entity of Tepheret. Netzah then sets the thing working while Hod relates it to the outside world. Yesod maintains its balance and gives it a view of itself. Malcut is what we see in its physical form when the Tree is complete, having brought the creative process down to Earth.

Some modern Cabalists insert the planet Uranus in the Sephira of Hochma. Though not universally agreed on, the notion contains some interesting ideas. Uranus was the father of Saturn, who dethroned him, early on in the making of the Universe. Uranus was the son of Gaea, the primal Mother Goddess, appearing after Chaos, at the beginning of Creation. Uranus was her first son. From their relationship came Saturn, her last born, who rendered his father impotent, and then was, in time, dethroned by Jupiter his own son.

Apart from a certain vague parallel with the Bible, perhaps more interesting is the fact that Uranus is the God of the starry cosmos—the seed bed of the Zodiac; also that he was considered by the Greeks as a primordial divinity and who together with his mother were considered the grandparents of the world. While not corresponding precisely with the Tree of Life there is nevertheless some interesting material to be thought about—and with any study of the Cabala the process never finishes. As in life, crystallisation means atrophy and death.

Modern Cabalists, as in the case of Hochma and Daat, ascribe for teaching purposes a god and planet to Kether. This

is Neptune, brother of Jupiter and God of the Sea. As powerful as Jupiter, he took up the rulership of the middle world of
water; with Jupiter above in the sky, and Pluto below in
the underworld. As a symbol of his power he carried a tri-
dent, perhaps a key to the three divine forces or trinity
which go to create the Universe. Another quality of Neptune
is, that like the sea, he is omnipotent; a presence like water
all over the earth. Some Cabalists see this as significant
and speculate on the flow nature of his being, referring to
the fact that he is the older brother to Jupiter. These ideas,
however, are only fragments of a larger pattern now lost,
and are probably distorted by time.

Traditionally the Sephira of Kether is described on this
scale as the Primum Mobile—the Prime Mover. This name
is more or less self-explanatory. But what moves, and who
moves it, is another matter; for it is more than an unseen
sphere singing as it rotates the seven heavens. Embedded in
the idea of the Primum Mobile is the same concept as in
Kether—the Crown. What streams through the Crown from
above is identical to that which lives beyond the Primum
Mobile. Perhaps it is pertinent to say at this point that above
the planetary, and above even the Prime Mover on this
scale, lie other Universes; three more in all. This accords with
the Cabalistic idea dealt with in the next chapter; that there
are four great Trees of Life, each one part of a vast chain
stretching from the Divine Universe, through the Creative
and Form Worlds to the realm of elements and action—
the one we live in. On this scale the scheme we have been
examining is in fact the lowest and densest universe; and
the planets observed in the sky are the tiny hard physical
cores of vast material organisations. We see the Sun as a
brilliant ball, but in reality we live inside its radiant body as
we do within the outer Van Allen radiation belts and atmosphere of Earth. Our planet does not cease to be, until well
beyond the Moon; and if we could view it with cosmic eyes

it would take the form of a vast pulsating tadpole with its diaphanous tail blown back by solar winds, rather than a solid and small blue and green sphere. This is the World of Assiah—the elements and action, the final stage of Kether when, at the end of the creative process, it becomes Malcut.

Here then is the Tree of Life laid out in terms of the old gods and the ideas they symbolised. By combining this with the corresponding knowledge and experience of the Sephiroth present in oneself, yet more insight into their nature can be gained. This is the practical application of the 'As above so below' principle so often quoted in ancient philosophy.

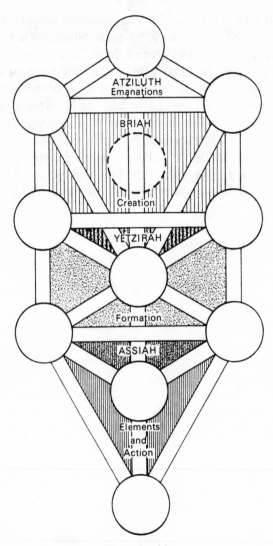

Four worlds

VII

The Four Worlds

Having set out the nature of the Sephiroth we pause, before exploring their relationships, to see how they fit into a yet grander design.

As there are four states of matter in the physical world—fire, air, water, and earth—so there are four corresponding levels within the relative Universe. Traditionally these are known as Atziluth—or world of Emanations, Briah—or world of Creations, Yetzirah—the world of Formations, and Assiah—the world of Substance and Action. These four realms form a chain of increasing density and number of laws the further they are removed from the Atziluthic world. Each level is a fainter mirror of the one above, until in the Assiatic world—the one we exist in—the materiality is so dense that we often only observe the surface of our environment.

In the great Tree of Life that composes all Creation these four worlds are set out in the general major horizontal divisions, of the Kether, Hochma, and Binah triad (Atziluth); the upper square formed by Hochma, Binah, Gevura, and Hesed (Briah); the lower square constructed by Hesed, Gevura, Netzah, and Hod, with Tepheret at its centre (Yetzirah); and the lower triad made up of Netzah, Hod, and Malcut, with Yesod at its centre (Assiah). Beginning at the top triad, these horizontal divisions roughly correspond to the four worlds. I say roughly, because it is also in the nature of these worlds to interpenetrate each other; not only on the Tree but literally, as heat does air, air water, and water earth.

Cabalists see the relationship between the worlds on the Tree in various ways, some see the demarcation in the horizontal, while others see it in the central triangles. Some for instance take Tepheret as the lowest point of the Briatic world, with Yesod performing the same role for the world of Yetzirah as it penetrates the Assiatic triangle.

This idea of the four universes is carried further in the notion that each world has its own complete Tree, so that the Malcut of the Tree of the Atziluthic world is the Tepheret of Briah world, interleafing on down to the bottommost Malcut where the residue of all the worlds is concentrated. This idea follows the rule that every complete unit in the Universe is based on the Tree. Moreover, it is said that within these miniature Trees the four worlds are repeated, and so on down to the smallest complete cosmos. This is quite different from the fact that within each individual Sephira there is another complete sub-Tree.

In man these four worlds correspond to different levels of his being. The lowest trial is the physical body, the lower square the realm of emotion, while the upper square matches the intellect. The topmost triad relates to the spirit. Various traditions have other names like carnal, subtle, rational, and divine bodies, but the meanings are much the same.

It is useful to identify these levels within oneself and one can easily observe them in any creative process or full human relationship. For instance in a love affair it sometimes becomes quickly apparent as to what is or is not there in spirit, head, heart, and gut. The predominance of one, or absence of another, quickly reveals itself. When all four are balanced the miraculous occurs.

Taking the World of Atziluth first this can be described, if at all, as the realm in which the Tree of Life is in its purest state. It is indeed functioning in the realm of emanations. Here, close to the Endless Light, all the Sephiroth are radiations or resonances directly in contact with the Divine.

Traditionally the Sephiroth are called by various God names, each one the purest aspect of the Absolute, as manifest in the relative Universe. From our distant view very little is known about them, and to pretend to this knowledge would be foolish. Mystical experiences are well known to be indescribable, not because of the lack of articulation on the part of the participants, but because there is no language or symbol adequate for illustration. It could be said to be like explaining Einstein's energy-mass equation to a sheep.

For those deeply interested in these names of power, as they are called, there is a great deal of literature. But this study does not require books; and to make contact with a master of the art is remote for anyone who has not been under a practical discipline for some time. Therefore I would suggest at this point we follow the brief set in this book, and observe the Tree of Life primarily at the Assiatic and perhaps the Yetziratic level.

The Briatic world, the realm of creations, is said to be of the universe of Archangels. These might be defined as intelligences that are concerned with the implementing of Divine instruction, and which set in motion the designing processes. At this level nothing may be seen, like the concept of a building long before even the sketch plans have been drawn. Here myriads of possibilities may be inherent. Out of one idea a whole new type of architecture may spring. This is the moment of creative activity before the formulation phase is set.

The Tree in the Briatic universe would describe the same operations as in the lower worlds, but the level of energy and materiality would be of greater potency; the Malcut of Briah containing elemental qualities that would make our most creative works crude and infantile.

The Yetziratic world is closer to our understanding. It is the realm of forms. Here the creative process is fluid and developing, like soft potters' clay while it is being worked.

At this point subtly manifests, endless variation and variety are possible, but within the context set up in the Briatic world. Here moulds are made and filled, changed and reformed. Here an ebb and flow occurs, configurations emerge and dissolve as they continually meet the requirements of a set of conditions. Yet always everything relates to the original concept. Many of man's arts are peepholes into the Yetziratic world, and his pursuit, for instance, of symbolism, is an attempt to fix this strange realm in Assiatic terms.

The Assiatic realm is composed of the elements. It is literally the world we live in. However, it is not quite as simple as pure physics, for the upper worlds permeate it. A cat originates from a thought in the mind of Nature in order to fulfil a cosmic need, as did the dinosaurs, and as men do now. From this view one cat is all cats, and all cats are but copies of one cat. Here we have a creative impulse originating in the Briatic world, and being manifested through its changing kitten, cat, corpse form, in the Assiatic world. If we ask the question what is a cat in the Assiatic world it is but the rearrangement of several hundred tins of cat food, plus air, water, and light. Solid as pussy is, she is not what she seems; nor are any of us in the Assiatic world.

So familiar are we with the phenomena of this realm that we tend to consider it as if it were the only one. The physical Universe, however cosmic it may appear, is only the face to the upper worlds, though in its reality it contains them all, for in Malcut is Kether, Spirit in Matter.

In the realm of Nature we see the ever-changing forms of flora and fauna. Here the elements move through an endless cycle only for a moment frozen in this or that plant or animal. But consider the construction of the millions of leaves in an orchard, and the original printed circuit for the exchange of energies needed, with the slow modification by mutation going on as the climate of the planet alters from ice to tropical age. All this is going on while men charge the atmosphere with radio waves, and with thoughts and feelings, not to mention the accumulation of the residue of generations of lives.

Above the world of Nature is the planet, and beyond this, the other planets, the sun, and the local star clusters. All these, including the Milky Way that we see stretched across the heavens on a clear night, are the world of Assiah. When we look up or down we see matter, and however slowly a galaxy may turn in comparison to our reference to time it is still in the realm of elements. Even the smallest atom belongs to the Assiatic kingdom, though its energy aspect may fall into the upper portion of the Assiatic Tree of Life.

Man lives in the Assiatic World. He does, however, have access to the upper Universes should he evolve and refine his being to be able to become aware of these realms. In order to do this he has to acquire more than the physical body Nature has supplied. He must organise out of the substances and energies permeating his being a new vehicle for each World. This takes time and work, knowledge and practice. It is said this is man's unique position. He can evolve as an individual. He has the possibility of rising above the gradual evolution of all creation and to surpass the angels and archangels, who, though of an initially higher order of intelligence, are fixed in their roles and function in the Cosmic Pattern. Man alone can by-pass the left and right sides of the Tree of Life and go straight up the middle column.

Looked at as a whole the four Worlds may be seen as four concentric bands, Atziluth on the outer ring, Assiah at the centre, each with ten ring divisions representing the ten Sephiroth of each world, based on the Pivot of Malcut within the Assiatic Circle. Beyond the outer periphery of the Kether of the Atziluthic world is the circumference of the Endless Light, and beyond this the other two veils of negative existence enclosed by the Absolute. Within the outer ring of the Atziluthic Kether the density increases each step inwards, the outmost ring or Sephira containing all the ones inside. In this way every link in this cosmic chain is ruled from above, while controlling those below. In terms of the density of vibrations the cyclic rates appear to increase the nearer to the centre we go, or the lower we descend; though in fact the subtler rates are present, but undetectable in, say, the Assiatic Universe. This interpenetration of the higher worlds into the lower might explain many things about the so-called 'next world', miracles, and other supernatural phenomena.

The different levels defined in this circular scheme of the Four Worlds were laid out by the Cabalists, at one point, into an evolutionary ladder called the Fifty Gates. This describes the progressive stages from Chaos, through the formation of the elements, to the Earth as we know it. It then proceeds to unfold the story of the rise of the vegetable kingdom out of the mineral world, then of animal life up to the vertebrate. Next the evolution of man is shown, with the step by step growth of his completion in the image of God. This is followed by a description of the heavenly spheres, from the Moon up through the planetary levels to the Empyrean Heaven beyond the Primum Mobile. After this the Angelic levels of the celestial hierarchies are laid out, with the last gate at the portal of Ain Soph, the End-less Light.

These cosmographs may seem quaint to us in modern terms, but it is perhaps more a question of language than accuracy. An angel, defined as a Cherubim, was quite differ-ent in nature and function from a Seraphim. This was in mediaeval times as precise a vocabulary as any in modern physics, perhaps more so. To us the symbolism may have no obvious meaning in our experience, or perhaps we call the same things by different names. However, the important thing to remember is that this scheme of the Universe was based on the same principles as the Tree. It was, for some, speculation, for others a working hypothesis, and for others perhaps a world either in imagination or reality. The same arguments apply to modern atomic physics and astronomy.

One final point. The Cabalist also sets out a mirror arrangement called the Qliphoth. This was the realm of demons or the world of shells. Caused by distortion, imbalance and atrophy, these were corresponding forces on every level of the Universe, but out of line with general evolution. Any organisation has these present, and they manifest when excess is reached either in over-activity or over-resistance. The symbol of shells indicates their fixity, their stop of flow, their separation from the living body. Thus, in human terms, a man who has lost contact with his humanity may become an officer in a Nazi concentration camp—a very demon! Similarly a country in civil war (the worst kind of war) is literally beset by archdemons, though we call them the forces of Communism or Fascism. The bitter Thirty Years War between Catholic and Protestant Europe illustrates how religious powers can become demonic. For different reasons a Qliphothic situation occurs when a country, or a man, stagnates in development. Historic inertia or traditional violence solidify into a rigid custom in a community, preventing economic growth or human rights, while corruption is tolerated. In a man such a hard psychological shell of lethargy or overactivity can strangle his personal evolution, and so prevent him from ever seeing the world outside his own fixed image of it.

All Qliphothic phenomena signify the disturbance of the natural interplay of the Sephiroth. The lack of, or over stimulus of the active or passive processes can create an imbalanced situation to a greater or lesser degree. Any permanent distortion in a Tree will generate a disastrous circumstance; on a large scale, global war, on the individual level, madness—indeed possession by devils.

Here then are the four Worlds, and the four horizontal

divisions of the Tree of Life. As said, for the purpose of this study we will mostly concentrate on the Assiatic world, so that by observing its working on our level we can perhaps glimpse into the upper worlds.

VIII

Triad and Octave

It is said that the relative Universe comes into existence through the interaction of two great laws. The first is the Law of the Triad Trinity which brings about an event, and the second is the Law of Octaves which shows the development of that event through a definite sequence. Both these laws are present everywhere, from the inception of Divine Creation down to the commonplace action of the striking of a match. Nothing can exist outside these two laws.

The concept of the Trinity is familiar in most major religions and philosophies, and the Cabala is no exception. In the Tree of Life it is seen very precisely in the Triad Kether, Hochma, and Binah. Here are the positive and negative factors shown in the pillars of force and form, with the third element of equilibrium bringing them into relationship in the central column. Nothing can happen until all three are in relationship, no more than a child can be conceived without the various conditions being right between a man and a woman. So it is throughout the Universe, wherever a real event occurs.

It will be noted on looking at the Tree that all the Sephiroth form themselves into triads. Moreover, every one of these triads is connected with the central column of consciousness. This is vital, for while the left and right columns are fixed in function (in the same way that a man is a man and nothing else), the central column completes any triad, thus enabling events to flow. It will also be observed

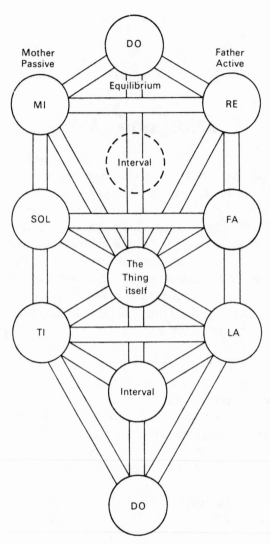

Triad and octave

that there are great triads and small triads in the Tree, and particular triads that relate principally to the central axis. All these have their special place in the cosmic scheme of the Tree, and most may behave in any one of six permutations which range through growth, decay, transformation, disease, renewal, and regeneration.

The Law of Octaves is based on the idea that between Kether and Malcut stretches a great string, a monochord, with the note Do at the top and bottom of the axis of consciousness. Here is another insight into the Cabalistic saying that 'Kether is in Malcut, and Malcut is in Kether'. From the view that this is a vast vibrating string, we may see that all other vibrations in the Universe are contained in this monochord; though they, however many, cannot compose it, any more than a billion people are a complete Adam. This monochord is of quite a different order. It is the Master Octave, while all the others are minor and mere harmonies to its great notes.

Like Jacob's ladder with the angels ascending and descending, the Octave has two main movements, up, and down. In music we see the principle of the notes becoming higher and of greater frequency as we move from Do, through Re, Me, Fa, So, La, Ti to Do. This is because the string is being shortened, and so more vibrations are being packed into a smaller pitch or space. In the Universe this takes on a great deal of meaning when we consider the wave and particle theories. As we descend towards the lower end of matter, density increases; that is, more particles are packed into a smaller space. Likewise when we look at vibrations— and these are interchangeable with the particles of matter —these appear to increase also, though not in the sense we usually understand high frequency. For it must be recalled that more beats imply a shortening of the string, bringing greater tension, but less flexibility. Here is a situation the converse of our normal perception of increased frequency,

for in fact any phenomenon in a high vibration zone is under
a greater constriction or more laws. The infinitesimal motions
and periods of atoms, as against the slower but more flexible
cell, describes very precisely the true situation of a materiality, where vibration is so compacted that nothing appears
to move. I repeat, appears, for what we normally think about
high vibration is that it is more powerful and free. As often
said, appearances can be deceptive and in the real Universe
often the reverse of what we see is the case. It is not without
reason man is sometimes viewed symbolically as contemplating the World upside down; seeing the transient as eternal,
and the eternal as transient. This is the first veil of illusion
we live in.

If we consider the Tree of Life in this light we shall
observe that the bottom Do of our usual view in fact starts
at the top, at Kether, and resolves in its maximum vibration
and compression in Malcut. To baffle us further the Octave
flows two ways, unwinding its intensity into the great monochord of Kether, having passed through the frets of the
Sephiroth. Both these flows occur simultaneously like a two-
way lightning flash joining Heaven and Earth in a single impulse, which in turn contains all the impulses of every level,
high or low down to the minutest movements of the atoms
of the densest metal. This is the raising of the Kingdom up
to the Crown, and the bringing of the Crown down to the
Kingdom, so that Heaven may manifest in Earth. The Law of
Octaves besides being seen in the one great progression from
Kether to Malcut can be observed on every scale, including
quite mundane phenomena such as the light spectrum, the
periodic table of elements, and of course as music. Using
the familiar tonal scale, but remembering to reverse the
apparent increase and decrease of frequency, we can plot the
nature of the Octave's development, when related to the
Tree of Life.

Striking the seemingly lower but in fact greater Do of

Kether the Octave moves down the path of the lightning flash to Hochma. Here, in its first manifestation, it enters the world of vibration at its initial fret or stop. Energy is now present. It then crosses to Binah the second note, where in the first passive Sephira it is slowed further and becomes locked in form, however rarefied it may appear to us. This is the first triad. From here, after an interval which we shall deal with in a moment, it flows on down through the Sephiroth of the Tree. It does not, however, appear to directly touch the central column again until it reaches the Do of Malcut. The reason for this is the peculiar law that determines Octaves.

After the Supernal triad of Kether, Hochma, and Binah, has set creation in motion there is a momentary pause, a slowing down that has to be bridged. This phenomenon is observable in any creative work in ordinary life, when there is an initial hesitance after a vigorous start. If this gap is not crossed, the action stops. Many books and pictures, well begun, have died at this critical point. What is needed is an impulse from outside to carry the movement over. In minor tasks often a walk, a conversation, or a coffee, act as the necessary stimulus. This boost takes the flow across to the note fa or the Sephira Hesed, the vital gap being filled by the invisible Sephira Daat which supplies the contact with the central column of conscious energy.

The Octave continues down the Lightning Flash follow-ing the development of the various Sephiroth, through Fa—Hesed, So—Gevura to La—Netzah. Here again it has traversed the central column of Equilibrium. By this time it has become apparent what the character of the octave is, and this nature is embodied in Tepheret. Anyone practising crea-tive work knows that once this point has been reached there is no changing. The essence of the book or picture is fixed. Only by beginning anew can any major discrepancy be cor-rected. Here again the third force—that of consciousness—manifests, but this time as the image of all the steps of the octave that have occurred, and will occur after; for the path is now already set and the result, except for details, crystallised. This is because all the paths feeding into Tepheret are now firmly focused.

After the nature of the octave has been determined the sequence continues, on through La—Netzah (cycles) to Ti—Hod (reverberation). Then it comes to the last interval, before completion. Here again this pause, often seen as heightened fatigue, is observable in quite ordinary tasks. A final major effort is needed to finish the sequence off. During the Second World War the British recognised this law at work in their war effort, and the B.B.C. put out two programmes of stimulating music at the times when it was known the factory workers were flagging. This may be a crude example, but it was a practical understanding of the working-day octave. In the case of the Tree this interval is filled by Yesod, the potent Sephira on the column of equilibrium. This vital centre completes three sub-triads in the big bottom triad of the Assiatic (action and matter) World thereby bringing the whole octave into full physical manifestation. In a book, this is the final labour of actually setting words down, and maintaining the flow over many weeks (no mean effort when it would be so easy just to think or talk about it). In Malcut the final Do is complete; and now Kether is indeed in Malcut, and Malcut in Kether.

It might be well to repeat here that between every note of an octave is a miniature octave, or to put it in Cabalistic terms, there is a complete Tree in and between each Sephira. This often accounts for why we cannot see the law clearly, for we only observe at most times particular notes, or Sephiroth. This could be because we have access to perhaps only one part in a complete process, like an editor who performs the Gevura-Hod tasks of the publishing sequence; or another example would be in the Law courts where we only see the Gevura-Binah function of the legal system.

The interaction of the two great laws of Octave and Trinity is manifold and gives rise to the many aspects of the Universe. In man their interaction is well demonstrated, and a trained eye can spot them at work. However, before we do our examination of the triads in relation to man, we must take note of certain subsidiary laws.

While in general the Male Column may be taken as the active principle flowing down into Yesod and Malcut and the Female column as the passive principle likewise joining there, it must be remembered the individual Sephiroth are subject to transvestism, that is, changing from negative to positive and vice versa. This is because of the fact that as the Lightning Flash descends, the upper Sephira always acts as the Active Principle to the recipient lower one, in the flow of emanations. For example: Hesed is passive in relation to Binah; and Gevura, normally passive, is active in this circumstance in relation to Tephereth. Moreover in each triad any one of the Sephiroth may take up an active, passive, or neutral status within a limited situation, that is, when operating in a minor role. This may or may not work in balance to the whole Tree. Such a malfunction in man, for instance, is when a Sephira which should be active is passive, or acting as the connecter. A good example of a passive Sephira usurping an active role is in the man who cannot get to sleep because his Hod cannot solve a problem outside its scope. The ordinary logical mind, becoming the active principle in the Hod, Yesod and Malcut triad, runs the question round and round in an endless loop drawing on data stored in the brain, which is seen as old and useless information on the Yesodic screen, offering no solution. Meanwhile in his restlessness the vitality level in the Netzah, Yesod, Malcut triad is dropping and quite unable to refresh the man because Netzah is rendered passive. The result is that there is not enough energy input from the active column of the Tree to lift him out of his locked situation. Eventually he falls asleep from sheer exhaustion. However, perhaps during the night when the Tree is functioning normally, his Gevura judgement can come into operation. If not, the night's rest, with Netzah performing naturally, will produce enough power in the organism to enable the man to tackle the problem in a balanced way next morning. Occasionally, as we all experience, solutions are produced by the upper Sephiroth during sleep, while the lower triads replenish the body and excrete waste mind matter through dreams. For the most part all the triads work well within a normal range of permutations checking and counterbalancing each other throughout the Tree, and these will be discussed later in detail after a general outline.

Taking the side triads first, these by their relationship to the force and form columns of the Tree are less flexible than those centred on the middle pillar. This is because the active and passive columns are more concerned with function than consciousness, and therefore have less freedom of action. This is easily spotted in a person who always makes value judgements (excess Gevura) or someone who has no self-discipline (lack of Gevura). However, they do have important jobs to perform. To take examples in man, the Hod-Yesod-Malcut triad defines the identifying processes, the memory and the body. Here is a continuous sequence of comparison. A story will illustrate some of the lower triads at work: While walking down the street a man's Hod is endlessly sorting out incoming impressions. He avoids a lamp post, reads a poster, negotiates crossing the street between three fast-moving cars, using conditioned reflex experience stored up in his Hod, Yesod, and Malcut triad. He knows where he is going, because over the years he has built up a picture of the district in this same triad, which can draw on the memory bank in the brain and flash a plan on his Yesodic screen at will. However, he sees an unfamiliar alleyway, and his Hod mind, ever-curious, directs his voluntary system to point his feet in that direction. On the other side of the Tree his Netzah-Yesod-Malcut triad tells him that he is hungry, that he ought to go home and eat. His Hod mind, intrigued by the new sights, smells, and sounds, ignores his hunger and prods him on. In the dim alleyway, on unfamiliar ground his Netzah, Yesod, Malcut triad adds a little adrenaline to his bloodstream. Already nervous, yet more stimulus is added by his Yesodic imagination, as he takes on the fantasy role of a secret agent. Brave, good looking and determined he presses on, feeling the make-believe pistol hard against his throbbing chest. Turning a corner his Hod-informed eyes dilate as he sees the silhouette of a girl standing in the shadows. Totally immersed in his illusion, his Yesod fills in the unseen face with idealised features, while his Netzah flushes a tinge of desire through his system. With his Hod, Netzah, Yesod triad suddenly excited, his sensual faculties are alert and his instincts expectant he approaches the girl half believing he will actually kiss her full and beautiful mouth. She turns abruptly and her face catches the light. It is old, hard, her lips are thin and dried. The Yesodic image vanishes, his Netzah is repulsed and his Hod quickly moves his Malcut body past her. The whole dream evaporates into reality. Realising that he is a fool he hurries on, groping his way back to familiar ground where after the momentary Self consciousness he once more drifts back into a Yesodic dream, this time about what he is to have for lunch, as his Netzahian hunger asks his Hod to guide his Malcut feet, with Yesod's help, home.

Taking a more perhaps serious line we leave these lower triads and examine those attached higher up the central column. Here taking again the example of man, we set out the traditional triads going up the pillar of consciousness.

Man is a half creature of the Earth. While living on the planet he is only partially under its laws. We read in the Bible that after his fall he was ejected from the Garden of

Eden into the world below. Here he was clothed in animal skins and on death was to be returned to the dust he was made of.

These are very interesting statements on man's origin and composition, especially when set out on the Tree of Life upon which we are told he is modelled after his Maker's image. Firstly his body is literally made up of dust or earth. It contains the vital fluids, uses air, and cannot live without heat or light. These are the elements as defined in Malcut. He is also alive in an organic form. In him are all the processes of the vegetable world. He eats, drinks, and breathes. He also grows and reproduces himself just as plants do. However, he is also an animal, with all the qualities of that realm. This makes him mobile, social, aggressive and loving, as well as many other attributes that are purely animal in their nature. The ideal family with every activity from the cradle, through childhood, courtship, marriage, home-making, career, to old age and the grave, are all part of the animal kingdom in man. Neither good nor bad, this is often seen as the human aspect of life, when it is not. The human element of a man is that he is conscious of himself, and knows that he is conscious. In this way he belongs to a very different kingdom from the animals.

The Tree defines the mineral level in Malcut, and the vegetable part of man in the great Hod, Netzah, Malcut triad. Here are all the bodily processes and circulations with the vegetable intelligence centred on the Hod, Netzah, Yesod triad. In this small trinity the cyclic processes are governed, from the responses to the outer world through Hod to the inner repeating mechanisms of Netzah. Yesod is the sex act or pollination. The Hod, Netzah, Yesod triad can also be called the 'Flesh', that is, it bears Life, as against a corpse.

The triad Hod, Netzah, Tepheret is the animal soul, or Nefesh, in traditional Hebrew, which refers to blood, or Life. This animates the body, gives it a higher level of con-

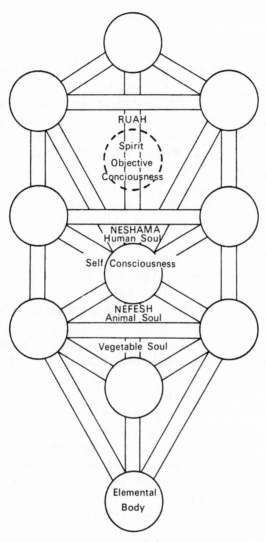

RUAH
Spirit
Objective
Conciousness

NESHAMA
Human Soul

Self Consciousness

NEFESH
Animal Soul

Vegetable Soul

Elemental
Body

Inner triads

sciousness even to the point that it knows it exists; but not that it knows that it knows. A cat is a very intelligent animal, but it is blind and deaf to anything outside its own sense of life. It may be curious about strange objects or creatures, but they play no part in its cat universe. It soon loses interest even in its own reflection and ceases to see it any more. Cats undoubtedly have dreams, as any cat owner will tell you. A cat undoubtedly possesses a Yesod, and growls and whines at the images the Hod, Netzah, Yesod triad circulates after a bad night with the local cat Mafia.

The Nefesh or Animal soul is by no means as inferior as implied. It has direct contact with Tepheret and is the next stage up on the vertical axis of consciousness. The complex made up of Tepheret, Hod, Netzah, Yesod and Malcut is a highly sophisticated organism with a clear identity though not necessarily to itself. A tiger is a distinct species, as is a cow. They are individualised examples of this configuration. However, a man is more than a species because he contains the ability to develop the whole Tree. This is possible by the next triad Tepheret, Gevura, Hesed which defines a man's self-awareness. In Hebrew this is known to most Cabalists as Ruah which is 'breath' or 'wind'. This no doubt refers to God breathing life into Adam. However, study of the oldest Text, the Bible in Hebrew (Gen II.7) reveals that the term Neshuma, or living human soul, is used, which is not of the same order as the Animal and Vegetable kingdoms. It is said that from the conception of a child to its birth the embryo passes through all the stages of natural evolution. Indeed it does, for it forms, out of the elements coming into the mother's body, a growing organism like a plant. It then transforms into a sea animal swimming in the womb fluids, before taking its first breath as a mammal. At what exact moment the human soul enters is still to be agreed though it is probably at the Tepheret point. It may be said, however, that a man's body on birth only contains genetic characteristics (the D.N.A. molecules in the cells carrying out the brief set by the chromosomes), but these are confined to the race and family of the man, not his psyche. If this were not true there would be no variety in any family. It is the Neshuma that makes a man an individual. It is his self-consciousness that separates him from the animal, and from most of his fellow men, who tend to conform with tribal (social-animal) practices and customs. The Neshuma makes the individual possible, because of its link with Gevura—Judgement and Hesed—Mercy. Here are emotional, human faculties; animals have no judgement or mercy. They do not kill their own species in conflict because of Netzah and the intelligence of Nature, which wishes to preserve the species. It is only highly developed animals such as apes or well organised societies like ants that fight; and this may be due in apes to the arising of the beginning of self-consciousness, and in ants to the fact that their society has mass intelligence greater than the individual ant. This is an area for study.

The Neshuma or soul, as we may also call it, pivoted on Tepheret has also access upwards to Kether. This gives it a unique point of reference and influx of energy. Any man truly in contact and centred in Tepheret is indeed self-conscious, for nearly all the paths focus there, though in ordinary men the upper ones may be just potential lines of communication.

The Bible implies in Gen I.2 that the triad formed by Hochma-Binah-Tepheret is the Ruah, the Breath or Spirit. Connected with the Divine triad this lower triangle pivoted in Essence may be called objective consciousness, that is, awareness of more than everything connected with one's self. Here is insight into the nature of the Universe. Things are seen not in a self-orientated way but in cosmic terms, larger than one's Self however noble or pure it may be. Rooted in Binah—Understanding, and Hochma—Wisdom, how else could it view creation? Moreover it interfaces with the

divine triad of Binah, Hochma, and Kether. This gives it a
direct relationship with the divine world, the Atziluthic
Universe of emanations. It is said by the Cabalists that on
death the Malcut body returns to the elements, Yesod soon
vanishing as the vegetable processes cease. That the Nefesh
remains while the vital energy triads slowly disintegrate
as the body decays. That the Neshuma or Soul finds its home
in an upper region, and that the Spirit, when the processes of
purification are complete, returns through Kether to the
Absolute.

The topmost triad is the Supernal Trinity. This is the
Divine World in man and Creation. From here streams the
three forces of the Trinity and the flowing sequences of the
Octaves and Sephiroth. The Cabalists further defined the
central triads into two main complexes. The upper one was
known as the great or long face and this was composed by
the Kether-Hochma-Binah-Tepheret form. Here the face
and beard of God reaches down through the Universe, each
hair carrying its divine instruction and existence. The lower
face was composed of Tepheret-Hod-Netzah and Malcut.
This was called the lesser face or lesser assembly. Here is
Adam or mankind. Between the upper and lower faces are
the Sephiroth of Gevura and Hesed, the Cherubim who stand
with flaming swords at the Gates to the Garden of Eden,
wherein walks the Lord God.

IX

Paths

The basic statement of the Tree of Life is that all is one, though there may appear to be many aspects, principles, and processes involved. From this it could be said that the Tree is a nuclear cell which divides up into the ten Sephiroth, through which flow the Divine Emanations setting in motion the interaction of the octave and trinity. All these become possible because of the paths forming the three columns and connecting every Sephira in a complex of circulation. Here is the original flow chart, but so designed that a whole series of Worlds can function.

The origin of the paths has been subject to much speculation. Some put forward the concept that the Tree is in fact a geometric solid with the paths between the Sephiroth marking the mid-zone division of balanced function. Thus Hesed and Gevura are separated but not parted. Others say that the Sephiroth were first formed, perhaps like crystals emerging out of a cosmic solution, and that the path patterns were the connecting rays of relationship. Yet others state that until two Sephiroth exist, a path between them cannot be born, while another school says that as the Divine Lightning Flash unfolds down its zig-zag the subsidiary paths follow making the secondary links.

All of these concepts are each in their own way correct, but perhaps the most significant fact for us is that some key has been lost. This explains why there are so many different interpretations of the paths by different schools down the ages. So here also is an area of study for our own time.

In order to demonstrate the state of understanding at this point a sample of views will be examined. What must be borne in mind is that the relationship between two Sephiroth not only includes the common element of both of them, but the path's position on the Tree, its place in that particular triad or set of triads, and which way the flow along it is moving. This it will be remembered is determined by the active, passive, or conditioning relationship of the three Sephiroth it is involved with. A complex analysis problem, but one that becomes easier with time and familiarity in the way that diagnosis does to an experienced doctor.

The first thing about the paths we have to know is that there are twenty-two of them. According of the most common system these are numbered, beginning after the tenth Sephira of Malcut, and start at the top of the Tree with the Kether-Hochma path designated as number eleven. The sequence then follows the enumeration across to twelve in Kether-Binah, then thirteen down to Tepheret and so on, until we reach the thirty-second path of Yesod and Malcut. This system is based on the three forces striking out from each Sephira as the Lightning Flash is unfolded, with the triads closed as the Flash sequence hits the adjacent Sephira on its descent. It is a logical development, though not every Cabalist would agree with it. It does show very clearly, however, a growth pattern, though it may be like an earthly lightning flash working from both directions simultaneously. Many people who use the Tree for personal development apply this particular system, identifying different paths by number and placing their own understanding of each connection between the Sephiroth. Such an example would be the path 31 between Hod and Malcut which would be concerned with subjects relating to science and the study of the physical world, as against path 23, Hod-Gevura, which would be perhaps an exercise in the development of critical discrimination about oneself. The significance of each path becomes more apparent as the Tree, particularly in relation to man, becomes known. Here we are only examining different ways of looking at the same phenomena.

It is said that the Sephiroth are objective and that the paths are subjective. In simple terms the Sephiroth always remain the same, like the position of the crown in England whose traditional cry is, on the death of a sovereign, 'The King is dead, long live the King'. This is no sentimental rite but the acknowledgement of a necessary constant which is above the fluctuations of time and governments. The Sephiroth are always the same in performing their function, If they did not, the relative Universe would collapse. A parallel analogue is seen in the constant elements forming a village society anywhere, and at any time. There are always the elders, the men and women, the adolescents and the children. Each person passes through different stages or initiations, be it in the jungle or on the city block corner, so that by maturity he has been the boy, the youth, the young married, the parent and so on. Almost everyone fills at some point one of these stations, either negatively or positively.

The paths are not constant in the same way as the Sephiroth. By nature they are subject to the two poles of the Sephiroth they are attached to. They also carry negative, positive, or natural charges, and take on the character required by the triads they participate in. They are like chameleons, but with definite colours, only able to assume a certain range of variants. This is, as the word 'subjective' implies, because they are not the rulers of a situation.

Many attempts have been made to synthesise the ranges covered by each path and this next system may be the oldest. We can guess, as speculation allows, that the Hebrew language may have been re-formed while the Jews were captive in Babylon in the 6th century before the common era. This was possible because Hebrew was no longer a first language but would become so, it was hoped, when the exiles returned to Palestine. Much work was done, not unlike the efforts of the 19th and 20th century Zionists who brought Hebrew into the modern world with new words taken from other contemporary tongues. In Babylon it was a different problem. The solution they were seeking (whoever they were who were behind this movement) was more than redesigning the Hebrew pictographs into Syriac letters. They were, it would appear, trying to restructure the actual root of the tongue so that it would act as a system within a system, as algebra does within the body of mathematics, but as applied to the five books of Moses, the Torah and the Tree of Life. From this sprang many later discoveries, and while some based on numerology were a very profound key to philosophy and the word structure of the Old Testament, many investigators became so enamoured with numbers and their meaning that they fooled themselves as well as many others. This is a phenomenon common to modern science as well, so perhaps one must accept these as failed experiments, along with the many unflying machines prior to the Wright brothers'. However, these dead-end journeys into numerical fantasy do not detract from the genuine work done by the early Rabbis who were making the most of a unique opportunity. The following is a glimpse into the research on their system being carried out at this present time. Like archaeology, only some of the foundations have been uncovered, and while we can only guess at the magnificence of the palace that lies buried we only have a wing or a courtyard at most at this point to work on.

The Hebrew alphabet has more than sound values. It also has numerical designations, symbolic, and cosmic meanings. The numerical values are simple and common to many ancient languages without a separate number system. Hebrew goes much deeper and has a whole metaphysic of allied numbers and families of words. This however is not our area

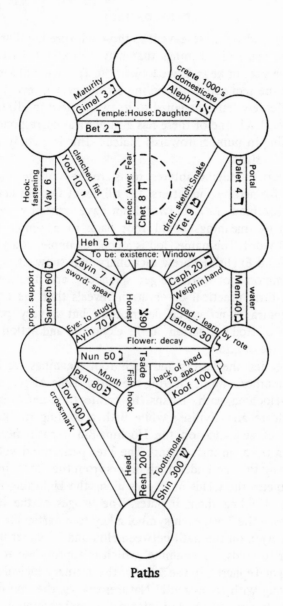

Paths

of study, and we must leave it to those who are familiar with the vast maze of meanings that may be extracted from so versatile a set of keys. If we look at the Tree we will see that besides the sequential numbering set out earlier, every path has a Hebrew letter assigned to it, twenty-two in all, of the alphabet. Each one of these has a numerical correspondence increasing in number towards Malcut. This is a study again in its own right.

Of more intelligible interest to us are the root meanings or images formed by the letters. Up till about the 8th century of the common era Hebrew did not have written vowels so that many meanings could root back to a simple three lettered word. The name Hod is a good example, as a glance through an English-Hebrew dictionary will show. It is from this common root word we get 'splendour' and 'to reverber- ate'. A little practical observation reveals that the title of this Sephira is no vague description, but a very precise account of Hod's function on the elemental and action level of the Tree of Life.

Examining the letters and their root meanings we begin to see another way of viewing the paths. Thus Aleph, in the Kether-Hochma path, means 'to create thousands', or 'to domesticate and civilise'; while Beth according to another system of sequence on the Hochma-Binah path means 'a house, a tribe, an instrument'. The Tree paths are developed further by this method, which differs from the others in that it completes the triads as it goes along the Lightning Flash, instead of filling them in later. The images of the letters flow down the Tree, each symbol a key to a particular path. So that Ayin on the path between Hod and Tepheret means 'eye, or to study, to examine' which is appropriate to Hod looking at Tepheret, in the sense of the ordinary logical mind conferring with its Essential Nature; that is, the one repre- senting Mercury, the god of information and communication addressing Apollo, the god of truth and illumination. This way of defining the different paths is very valuable, and there is reason to believe from current research that a whole city of philosophy is to be dug out of the roots of the Tree and the ground beds of Hebrew. For instance a way of read-ing the paths based on this system of lettering gives some interesting insights. The Netzah, Malcut, Hod triad and their respective letters Shin, Nun, and Tov, form the root word of 'cycles, day, year, and sleep' etc. The triad Hod, Netzah, Yesod forms by their letters Nun, Koof, Peh, the root of the words 'to go round in a circle'. Hod, Netzah, Tepheret and their path letters form the root of 'lock in position, to be shod'. The letters of the Gevura, Hesed, Tepheret triad form the word Zayin, Caph, Heh, which is the root of 'purifica tion, or cleanse' in all its senses. Binah, Hochma, and Tepheret and their letters Yod, Tet, Beth form the root of 'to make fertile, to improve'. The last triad Kether, Hochma, Binah which give the letters Gimel, Beth, and Aleph, means 'reservoir of water, or underground system'. Incidentally, Adam derives from Kether, Hochma, and Hesed, the letters meaning 'blood living, red, and man'. The letters of the Netzah, Malcut, and Malcut, Hod triad form Seth the son of Adam—which also means 'the basis or bottom'. Finally the path letters from Hod, Gevura, Gevura, Binah, Binah, Kether, spell out Samech, Vav, Gimel which means to 'return to source', thus completing the whole cycle. While of advanced academic interest, these root words and letters given an insight into the detail infrastructure of the tree to be explored.

Yet another facet to the Hebrew alphabet are the planet-ary, zodiacal, and elemental designations given in the ancient Book of Formation. In this early Cabalistic work the letters when set out in the second sequence also describe, according to the letter and its correspondence, the nature of the paths. Thus the path between Malcut and Yesod let-tered Resh is the path of Saturn which is a long hard rise, in human terms, through the material world of forms. Here is an earthy intelligence, the patience-creating experience of seeing the Universe behind the outer surface of existence. This is a tough, gloomy path, but one that develops strength and resilience. Here we have yet another key to the nature of the path, though the language of planets and zodiac may not be of our time. This creates many difficulties for those studying the Tree of Life, for the centuries of residue on work, once so alive in its day, now only obscures the view. Ideas and symbols sometimes outlive their usefulness. If they are real archetypes they return in modified form, like the eternal Venus of each generation who reveals herself quite clearly despite changing fashion.

A third system that is related to the Tree and paths and is worth examining (even though it has been dimmed not so much by time, as by superstition) is the Tarot pack. This is a collection of cards that first appeared in the Middle Ages. Today we only have the anaemic minor pack in the form of ordinary playing cards, and several beautiful but probably incomplete versions of the major set.

Time, the remaking of new blocks, fashions, and men adding their own ideas to the cards, have for the most part left us only a fragmented image of what the pictures were like. As a system it is impressive with its graphic symbolism, but there is something missing. However we have reason to speculate that the Tree of Life is the frame of reference needed to complete it. Here are some possible clues.

The minor pack is composed of four suits, each made up of ten numbers beginning with the Ace. If we read the four suits as diagrams of the four worlds or universes, we have a Diamond or Pentacle for Assiah, Hearts or Cups for Yetzirah, Spades or Swords for Briah, and Clubs or Wands for the Atziluthic world. Here we have Earth, Water, Air, and Fire again. Moreover, in the four royal cards attached to each suit we find the four levels contained within each world-suit

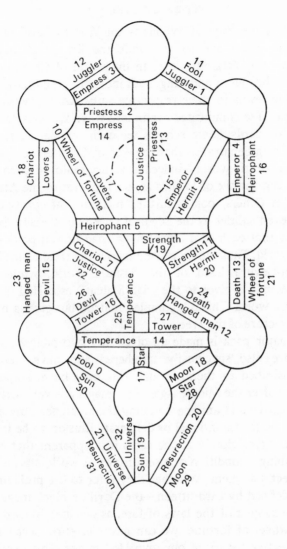

Tarot: two systems

Tree. Thus the Page of Wands is the Assiatic level in the Atziluthic world and so on, while the Knight of Swords represents the Yetziratic level in the world of Creation. So it is with the Queen and King, both indicating the Briatic and Atziluthic levels in their respective suits. Kinship with the Cabalistic Tree is indicated even more when we consider the suit of ten cards. Some schools see each number as corresponding to a Sephira, so that the Ace of Cups is the Kether of the Yetziratic world—indeed a watery realm of changing forms—and the six of Wands as the Tepheret of the Atziluthic realm. Others, looking further, maintain the correspondence is even subtler as the Sephiroth are not so easily fixed. They say that each card represents a triad in that particular suit or world. Thus the six of Pentacles is the triad formed by Tepheret-Gevura-Hesed of the Assiatic world, while the ten of Wands is pivot to the triad Malcut-Yesod-Hod in the Atziluthic world. This is a complex matrix, but gives a more definite picture of the Tree.

The major pack is made up of twenty-two picture cards. These are also specifically numbered and have Hebrew letters ascribed to them, though this may have happened before or after the Middle Ages. The imagery is very strange and evocative and anyone handling them can see how easy it would be for intentional or deliberate illusion to be introduced. Looking closely at the cards it is apparent that each is describing a condition or a set of laws at work, a principle or a direct statement. Whether they refer to the problem of lies, as defined by card fifteen—the Devil or black magician —or the subject of the laws of fate, as outlined in card ten or the wheel of fortune, we can never be sure, because of the subjective nature of our own Hod minds. This exercise must be left alone until we have the key to follow this particular method—which to the over-imaginative and spiritually gullible only leads to intriguing, fascinating cul-de-sacs. Here we will look at them in terms of the Tree to illustrate how careful one must be when speculating with old material.

There are several systems whereby the twenty-two major Tarot cards may be placed on the paths of the Tree. While there may be a certain amount gained by such study, the very fact that independent and extremely intelligent versions have been set up on the paths makes the whole operation suspect. This does not invalidate the effects of the two illustrated examples, it merely shows just how subjective the paths are, therefore I advise the student of the Cabala to examine and learn from the Tree in its and his own terms, and in words and images of his own time.

It is said that the Tarot pack was a philosophical machine that when arranged in different ways could answer all questions, be it about the nature of the world, man, or God. We have now reached a point in our study where we can see that the Tree of Life is possibly a similar machine. Here we have a superb frame of reference, cosmic in its scale, divine in its reasoning. We may use it as men have done down the ages to look at our own times, see from the point of the eternal, the ephemeral world. The Tree of Life is perhaps one of the subtlest inventions in our modern world despite its great age, and I would think its devisers would take it as a compliment for the title 'Machina philosophica' to be updated to 'Cosmic computer'.

X

Practice

We have now completed our brief theoretical study of the Tree of Life. There is much more to be learned about its nature and mechanics, but this can only be acquired through time and practice. The practical application of the Tree is most important, for while we learn through Hod we must balance it with Netzah. In this way both columns of the Tree come into action, pivoted and observed from the central pillar.

The Tree of Life is a tool and a technique. It may be used in many ways, ranging from attaining full personal development to examining a relatively worldly body such as Parliament. From its scheme various psychological and physical disciplines can be planned. By obtaining understanding and mastery of the various aspects of the Tree extra power may be acquired, and perceptions opened into new worlds. These practices, however, require a skilled and reliable teacher, who though unusual in spiritual calibre must be quite normal in his relation to the everyday world. A gifted but impractical instructor is not only useless, but dangerous. One does not go mountain climbing with a guide who is even mildly unbalanced.

In a book such as this any attempt to show the Tree at work must be modest. Here we can only use the dim reflection of words to illustrate its potential. Therefore in this latter section we will look at various complete organisms and phenomena, to see how our cosmic microscope can throw light on to anything placed on the slide plate of Tepheret.

First we must set the rules for what can be examined. The prerequisite is that it is complete, that is, that it is an entire entity and not part of a unit. The heart is not such an object, it is big and important, but only a nodal point in one of many cycles in the body. Nor is the body complete. At death the vital forces depart and the body ceases to function, quickly disintegrating back to its elements. Only a living man is complete. But we must remember that what we see walking down the street is just a thin momentary visible slice of his life. The rest exists, all his past and future ages and experiences are there present, but out of sight, beyond Malcut.

To examine any subject we must first define what it is, identify its essence. Thus with a man it is that which is peculiarly his, and with him from the womb to the grave. Having seen this nucleus, we place it on the Sephira Tepheret. This is the main focus of our cosmic instrument. From this sharp image we can establish the other aspects in their respective Sephiroth. Having set the field of view, the relationships of the different parts of the whole become apparent. The Lightning Flash describes how the subject is formed; the central triads, the various inner levels, and the side triads reveal the different interactional functions, while the paths show in detail the interchange with the shifts of balance. This study will sometimes indicate a flaw and its remedy. The conclusions made from a session at the eye-piece of this extraordinary cosmic tool will often change the observer's view of the subject for ever, for it is a curious fact that having once seen quite mundane things in so deep and wide a glance, nothing ever appears as trivial as it did before.

We will begin the series of examinations with a look at the parliamentary system, because it is a quite easily recognisable human pattern. Accompanying each Tree will be a commentary, by no means full, but enough to show a method of working. Later studies will be the examination of events and phenomena to show the application of the Tree in other ways. Finally, we will take again a look at man, aware that we are in ourselves a Tree, a perfect living instrument in our own right.

XI

Exercise

To anyone who has read so far and wishes to know more, it is important to realise the word Cabala means 'to receive'. However, there are four possible ways to understand the same communication. They are the mystical, the metaphysical, the allegorical, and the literal. Here are the four worlds and their keys. In order to practise unlocking doors I suggest as an initiation an exercise. This will perhaps place things in a personal context.

Find a quiet place, and sit comfortably with your spine straight.

This is Malcut.

Place your hands on your knees and close your eyes.

This is Hod.

Feel your pulse and breath.

This is Netzah.

Watch the images pass endlessly before your mind's eye.

This is Yesod.

Centre your attention away from the outer scene and the inner pictures and sensations, and focus on that part of you that watches this all happening.

This is Tepheret.

Here is the lower face of Natural man. Above, on your own Tree of Life, is the upper face or the Supernatural man.

When you have become quiet and composed, the soul turned towards spirit, you may become one with yourself. Then you are indeed ready 'to receive'.

Practise this at least once a day.

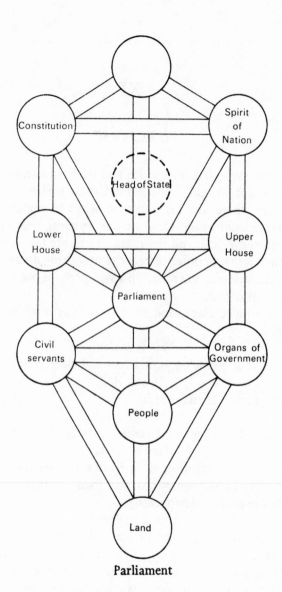

Parliament

XII

Parliament

The idea of a parliament is a very ancient one. Every primitive tribe, anywhere on the planet and in any age, has had its head man, its elders, and laws designed for the common good of that community. Examining our modern parliamentary systems, providing they are not completely totalitarian —and even these have an underground Gevura opposition— we see how the Tree of government functions, often unknowingly, in accord with cosmic principles.

Kether the crown in this study may be several things. Besides its fountainhead position it can be the civilisation itself —of which a nation is a sub-culture—with its Christian or Buddhist ideal, or even a physical Utopia of Communism. Both spiritual and material heavens indicate a direction, an upper realm for that nation. Kether may be Humanity itself, the Unity of all men to which the nation is joined in common bond. This could be confined to those at present living on the Earth, or all the ancestors and descendants yet to come. Either way Kether is of vast import, the Creative emanations flowing down in generations to become manifest as a dynamic in Hochma.

In Hochma is the Spirit of a people. We see over long periods of history how national communities have distinct characteristics like a person. This people, for example, are inventors, that warriors, while those are religious by inclination. All nations contain everything human, but one or several traits dominate its history, though from time to time these will ebb and flow in strength. The English for instance have a remarkable aptitude for invention and discovery. It is not without reason the Industrial Revolution began in England, where the Malcutic elements of coal and iron were exploited by this practical people. The Jews, for example, perhaps because of their long literacy, have certain intellectual skills whose abilities are not only used in the market place, but in scholarship, medicine and government. A nation of wanderers, they were, and are, often to be found as advisers, but never leaders in their host country. The Scots, another scattered people, are intelligent, tough and serious with a particular talent for pioneering, while their fellow Celts, the Irish, just as tough, are easy-going fighters and talkers.

The national image of a people, though often a distorted caricature, roots back to the spirit of the nation. This spirit is more powerful than is generally imagined. Not only does an Englishman become more English when he is abroad, but one may recognise the power of his culture wherever the English have been, be it India or north America. King Arthur, Sir Francis Drake, Wellington; all embodied the spirit of England in their time, and Churchill drew on this same spirit in 1940 and used its power to reinforce the British bulldog image. This may be regarded as old-fashioned thinking in the present time, but bring any people under pressure and the Hochma of that nation will speak with a powerful voice.

The Binah on this Tree is the formulation of the tribe's character and needs into a set of mores or customs. In a sophisticated society this becomes the constitution. In the case of England which has a thousand years of continuous development, beginning with a relatively primitive installation of a Conqueror (1066), the process has never been fixed, while in comparatively recent times the American constitution was drafted at one historical point, though it is still being amended. Both these written and unwritten constitutions fulfil the same function. Situated at the head of the passive side of the Tree they make the powerful national energies conform. Without law there would be anarchy, and the community as a whole would suffer. Therefore the Binah operation for the common good is vital.

This Sephira may in a primitive tribe be the crudest and most superstitious form of constraint, but it will safeguard the tribe and guide it through internal and external difficulties, though it will be amended as the community progresses. Men will fight and die to defend Binah, though they know nothing of its purpose beyond a general principle. The English Magna Carta, though of no particular benefit to commoners, has been held up by the Englishman as a symbol of his rights for seven centuries. In it he recognises the written declaration of his protection under the law. Here is the constraining yet beneficial quality of Binah, for while it creates duties it grants privileges; thus we get a phrase in the Declaration of Independence: 'We hold these truths to be self evident, that all men are created equal.' Here is the American dream—and nightmare. This is the scale of Binah. Placed opposite to Hochma it is concerned with great principles, not petty rules.

Following the Lightning Flash we cross the invisible Sephira of Daat. This position is occupied by the Head of State who is theoretically above the ordinary law. In England the sovereign holds the position of constitutional monarch, rather like a crowned president. Being based upon ancient custom it shows its root. The Monarchy is on the main axis of the Tree. It has vertical and direct connection with the parliament, and thereby the people. As ruler, Daat originally held the land, represented by Malcut, given by God, signified by Kether, for the people, identified by Yesod. Tepheret literally being the meeting place on the tree is also parliament. The Throne indeed had divine right, but it was not quite how Charles Stuart interpreted it. His duty was to protect the people from bad government, but not take the power and wealth of the Nation for himself, as did Louis XIV. Both kings generated revolutions.

In England a bill only becomes law on the sovereign's assent, the Crown's theoretically direct contact with Kether relating it to Divine Will. That is why governments may fall in Britain, but Parliament continues. The Crown, embodied in this or that sovereign, was, as in ancient China and Japan, connected with heaven. This gave the royal prerogative of mercy, and many other privileges traditionally granted to heads of state. The pale residue is still present at coronations, inaugurations, and state occasions. Anyone who witnessed the funeral of President Kennedy was seeing more than the burial of an Irish immigrant's great grandson.

Daat is the mystique of royalty, the curious aura surrounding a president. The people no longer see the human being, but sense the presence of something closer to the divine than themselves. The President and the Queen fill a position which possesses magic. Anyone who dons the robe of head of state has to appear, if not be, perfect. The invisible becomes visible in the embodiment of that person. As individuals they vanish, in the way that a spiritually developing man who reaches this point in himself disappears into Kether. This is the quality of Daat.

Hesed is seen in the upper house of any parliament. In England it is the Lords, in the United States the Senate. Even those countries that have a single chamber have an upper court, through which must pass any bill before it is made law. These are the elders of the tribe, the aldermen, who, being men of tried worth and experience, may check to see if the lower chamber is working in the community's interest. With their position on the Tree they have access to Hochma, the spirit of the nation, and while they do not draft the laws they are expected to refer to the genius of their

country as a check, and modify unjust or expedient legis-
lation. Often composed of older men who are usually
past the zenith of their political ambition, their view
is less biassed and more generous. In England this is the
highest court in the land, though still beneath the authority
of the Throne. Here are men and women gathered from a
wide range in life. Originally the Lords Spiritual and Temporal, their ranks now include trade unionists, judges,
industrial magnates, and even actors and writers. Here in
England, which is perhaps the most politically mature
country in the world, archbishops argue moral points with
journalists on an equal footing, both aware that in the House
of Lords they are the long-view guardians of the unwritten
British constitution. The quality of the upper chamber is
greatness, and all the attributes of Hesed. Even in the Soviet
Union this Sephira is recognised, as the people sense instinctively there must be a higher court even in a one-party
State.

The lower chamber in the British system is the House of
Commons. This demonstrates very clearly the nature of
Gevura. It is a place of contention—how else could it be
with a two or more party system? The British actually pay
an M.P. to be the leader of the opposition. His job is to test
the government's policy, seek every chink in its armour,
hack off bad pieces of a bill, smash anything the opposition
considers unjust while the party in power has to defend its
proposals. This is the Sephira of Mars. Here is the ordinary
outer emotion of a man. This is the Aye and Nay, the mundane judgements, the assessments, the point of decision with
each clause argued out across the floor of the chamber. There
is even a semi-military protocol in most Parliaments, rules
of debate, so that the verbal conflict does not become a
physical riot. Bitter exchanges are reported in the press as a
government wins or is defeated. The atmosphere occasionally
gets extremely emotional, and in some more volatile

countries tables and chairs fly across the chamber. In Britain they actually have a Sergeant at Arms who escorts any miscreant, be he an M.P. or a member of the public, from the chamber. This is Gevura, but in control; that is, beneath the direct influence of Binah above. Under rule the lower house works well, always referring to the constitution, and checked by the upper house opposite, in Hesed. It is here the laws are hammered out in detail, be it in the chamber proper or in committee. However, while the commons or congressmen may determine which way a policy will go, it is still finally subject to the rest of the Tree.

Tepheret is Parliament. It is all the pomp and pageantry, the authority and the power of the country seen in its parliamentary building set in the middle of the capital city. Here is the central focus of political power for the rulership of the state. Usually impressive in architecture it must be seen to function. Beside the everyday customs that reveal its authority, such as the House of Commons not being able to begin its business till the Mace, the symbol of parliament, is in its place, so the Sovereign must open each session. The Queen's ride in a coach, surrounded by lifeguard horsemen, is not a parade for tourists. Her short journey from Buckingham Palace to Westminster is part of the Tepheret activity of Beauty. Situated on the middle column at the point of many intersections, the opening of Parliament finds the building jammed with Lords and M.P.s, distinguished visitors, and many other people privileged to be there. These occasions bring all the Tree of the government of Britain together, with the Sovereign seated on the throne representing the presence of the continual line of history as manifest at that moment. Tepheret is, in the Lightning Flash or Octave, the Thing itself. Under our cosmic microscope it is Parliament, an object which is not just the Palace of Westminster or the people in it. Nor is it the quaint customs, or uniforms; neither is it the statute book nor the political parties. It is all these things, both particular and general. Its quality runs through the meaning of government, so that it shines like the Sun—bright or dim over a whole country, bringing detriment or benefit according to the intelligence of its electorate.

Netzah is all the organs of government. In Britain these are the departments and ministries, also the services, and all those organisations concerned with running the country. Generally, as in the case of the tax collectors, their function is cyclic, often coinciding with the seasons. The Board of Trade, Ministries of Agriculture and Fisheries are good examples. Some departments may be concerned with power, while others administer the Nationalised coal and steel industries. Yet others run the country's railway system, while another Ministry will take care of the environment and pollution. All these are Netzah activities, the involuntary process required to keep a living body, or the economy, healthy. This includes the defence services who, like white blood corpuscles, are designed to protect the national organism from invasion. Any country that allows its defences to weaken, unless it has a powerful ally, soon dissolves and is absorbed by another. History is full of such stories: the Roman empire eventually collapsed because of internal corruption—or disease. The vitality of a country is contingent on its wealth and vigour, that is on an economic sub-Tree of Life which supplies the bounty of resource. The power in wealth and people gives the Foreign Office or State Department its authority and military weight in the world outside. No one listens to a poor country's cause, however just.

Netzah is the machinery of government, the interdepartmental machinations. The Ministry of Pensions pays out, whatever party is in government. The Post Office, except when it is on strike, keeps—like the state radio—the nervous system of the nation going. The daily delivery of electric and gas bills, licences, and a dozen other public demands, are just links in a national Netzahian chain of cycles vital to the country's well being.

Hod in the Tree of government is its civil service. These are the mercurial data gatherers, the myriads of forms sent out and returned to collect a vast amount of information varying from your income to a full census on the whole community. The material netted by this constant casting is stored, at least for a year, until it is out of date. Here are the great banks of files on social security, health, legal, and financial matters. With the government computer, the Hod element is complete.

Other Hod activities are the official communications. This can range from leaflets to know how to claim a tax rebate, to simple political propaganda. The publicity campaign on the decimalisation of the British pound is a good example.

Special departments designed to deal with specific problems come under Hod. These may advise companies concerning trade abroad, or give information about new towns planned, or areas to be opened up. Advisory bureaux at all levels of administration come into this Sephira, as do index systems, and the access to facts only a large concern like a government can afford to investigate. These would be sections that look at new inventions, like the Royal Aircraft Establishment or N.A.S.A. and many other investigatory bodies. Many of these would be linked with the Universities, who of course also fit into the Hod activity of the country.

Obvious functions such as the country's telecommunications relate to this Sephira, and so do the links with the outside world, including the secret services like the C.I.A. Here are the customs and excise, the emigration sections, as well as the government-sponsored trading missions and trade fairs. Her Majesty's Stationery Office is pure Hod, as is any government white paper. Every letter bearing the cypher 'On Her Majesty's Service' belongs to this activity, as does the despatch box sent to the Queen containing documents for her attention. For as said, until the royal signature is signed and sealed, it cannot become law, but remains Hod.

Civil servants often draft bills well ahead of their times. This is because with their analyses of information they can anticipate what a minister may want. These are frequently worked out in detail, only to be modified on the floor of the House of Commons. Here is Hod in service beneath Gevura, although its loyalty is primarily towards the incorruptible parliamentary ideal of Tepheret.

Yesod is the people. Like their planetary counterpart, they are as the moon. Heavy, they change from time to time, sometimes reflecting, sometimes reacting to circumstance, be it parochial or international. The people on this scale are similar to the sea, their tidal mood putting that government in and throwing that one out of the parliament house, leaving it perhaps high and dry halfway through what it thought was to be the second leg of a good term of office.

Yesod is the realm of dreams and mirages, and the politician knows that his public image will make or mar his career, with every TV interview and speech on the hustings affecting his chances to become a Prime Minister or President. An aspiring candidate takes great care to build up a good Yesodic picture of himself, slanting it to show he is aware of the man in the street and his problems; though once in power, his eye is on different matters. All the political campaigners over the world know that there has to be excitement in order to move the masses even to vote, unless they are forced to exercise their right by law. Bands, meetings, even a little heckling and fighting, will at least generate some wave motion in the population. The people on the whole are passive, living their daily round much the same, only occasionally stirred by a major condition such as war or depression. For the most part they read the papers, watch TV, hear the news on car radios, unmoved, except when it personally involves them, and when some catastrophe occurs elsewhere, it soon passes from the Yesodic screen of the nation, fading into the ever-changing cycle of work, play, and sleep. The people are the power of the nation. Their endless generation supplies the energy to work the natural wealth. From this generating point come the men and women who rise up, for whatever reason, be it ideals or personal gain, into the Tree of Parliament. It is this Sephira that supports parliament, yet must be governed by it, so that it does not fall into anarchy. The laws are made to contain, but protect the people, so that the meanest individual has justice though it be he versus the Crown in the lowest or highest court in the land.

Malcut is the land. It is the earth itself, the rivers, lakes, and the surrounding seas. It is the air above, and the right to the sky. Before men came, England was an island wilderness. Here the natural laws of the jungle were at work. On man's arrival the balance changed, the forests and marshes were cleared, and the mineral wealth of the land exploited. Whether this is good or bad is not for us to judge, for we must see man's contribution from a planetary level to see the whole. All that can be said is that man is the spearpoint of evolution, and his pushing back of the wilderness part of a cosmic design—pollution, when corrected, included. From our Parliamentary Tree stand-point, we can see how it is literally rooted in the soil. Men cannot live without land. Food may be brought in, but space he must have, to live and work. Here we see how in Britain the Crown holds the land, a gift from God, for the people. Over the years this has appeared to have become a mere symbol. But in fact, we see, with the evolution of social conscience, that both capitalist and communist societies recognise that the duty of the Parliament is not to the political or wealth-orientated aristocracy, but to the people as a whole. Here once again the inherent Tree of a complete organism asserts itself. If it does not—and we witness again and again throughout history the results when governments do not allow the natural flow of the Tree—revolution breaks out, and there is an attempt to set up a balanced order again. This does not therefore recommend revolution, because in violent storms the Tree of Life shakes, like any other, disturbing its equilibrium. For example : Sometimes the people rise up and mob rule, like the Yesodic nightmare of the Reign of Terror in Paris, takes over the government. Occasionally a man in the position of head of state actually begins to believe he is God rather than His steward over a Nation. More than one dictator has fallen on this one. In most cases of crisis one side of the parliamentary Tree is too heavy; so that we get a government or over-Hesed action like that in pre-Revolutionary France, on the Force column, or a state run by Gevura-Puritans as in Cromwell's England on the Form side.

Here then, as our first exercise, is the Parliamentary Tree of Life. The same technique may be applied to a commercial company or a university or any complete organisation.

XIII

God and Mammon

In this exercise we take two Trees simultaneously in order to study parallel principles. Here we also follow how the Tree develops and establishes itself at each level. Taking the two poles of celestrial and terrestrial wealth we set up a contrast, showing how even Mammon has to obey cosmic law.

Beginning with the financial Tree, we take Hochma as the first manifestation. Here is born the concept of a token of exchange. This is a global idea common to all but the most primitive communities. The notion of money is a powerful abstraction, requiring an appreciation of a level well above exchange and barter. This is the creation of a symbol, be it metal, shell, stone, or paper, which makes possible a complete flexibility of transaction. By the mutual acceptance of currency many new things are possible for a tribal economy. A large community with different peoples exchanging multifarious goods and skills can grow larger still. Men may pay for services they themselves cannot perform with currency earned by their own particular talents. Without money, that vital, neutral, but commonly valued token, modern civilisation could not have evolved. Money is one of the three forces in the economic triad of activity. Principally the intermediary, it may also be the activator, or the result. Which ever way, the first tribesmen who saw that a form of money was the solution to the exchange of goods and services problem opened up a vast new field that was to affect mankind greatly. This glimpse of a principle perhaps came from a profound insight into the cosmic law of work and payment, which runs throughout Creation.

Taking the same Sephira but on the Tree of Philosophy, Hochma would be the enlightenment of a Teacher. Here the Flash of illumination coming down from Kether reveals the intention of the Divine. The Teacher may have received this insight in one brilliant illumination, or a succession of such moments over a lifetime. Aware at the level of Wisdom or inner intellect he perceives the Will of the Creator in everything, and sees the Universe and men permeated through with emanations. To humanity the teacher appears to be the fountainhead, the human radiance through which flows the glory of God. The Master, situated at the position of Hochma, sends out through the three succeeding paths the driving force of a profound philosophy or world religion. Men look to him as the representative on Earth of God, or the exponent of divine wisdom. He is the ideal, the Prophet, the Buddha, the Messiah, the source of the inspiration.

The tradition based on his teaching is formulated in Binah. Here, with understanding, the sayings of the Master are ordered into precepts. St Paul spent his life doing this for Christ. Based on the Teacher's life, a whole set of outlooks are evolved. The Master's view of the Universe is rationalised and his position in the cosmic hierarchy fixed, even if there is no obvious ladder of evolution. It is at this point that the various eightfold paths, thirteen principles of faith, and ten commandments are laid down. It is here that the organisation of the religion begins, and the rituals, customs and practices of that tradition are worked out, though perhaps over hundreds of years. Binah, being the passive mother Sephira, imbues the tradition with all the conservative, submissive qualities common to each religion or philosophy. Nothing must be changed. Occasionally, when the form pillar is too active, orthodoxy becomes sometimes as powerful as the Master's word, sometimes more so, so that men trying to relieve the original Master's way are destroyed by his Church. This happens when the letter of the Law becomes more important than the Spirit; in Cabalistic terms when the passive Binah becomes active. This usually occurs long after the Master has taken his physical departure and his followers fearing to lose contact preserve the outward form rather than the essence of his teaching.

In the Tree of Economics Binah is the formulation of the principles of finance. Here, well respected rules must be set up, so that transactions on a scale larger than the village market place are possible. A high level of trust must be created, and facilities for lending and borrowing (to offset time lag between outlay and profit) be made available. This requires organisation; the setting up of a banking system with its numerous checking points and receiving and distribution centres. Good reliable communications are vital, and the type of men involved in running such a system must have unimpeachable reputations. The different levels of commerce ranging from local to national have to be identified, also the recognition of various kinds of activity on the economic ladder. A whole picture of the state of industry, the stability of a community has to be assessed, so that calculated risks with a view to profit and economic development can be sponsored. The effect of this system has to be taken into account, for by nature it must be conservative to maintain its reliability, yet speculative enough to expand. Banking traditions grow, and the men running the institutions are expected to conform to the financial house's image. No national or international banking concern can afford big mistakes, besides there are the mutual obligations to other banking organisations, all of which form a global financial system.

In financial terms Hesed represents wealth, be it in hard currency, gold, oil, goods, or national skills. Britain, for example, is a trading as well as a manufacturing nation. Her wealth is not just the gold stored in the Bank of England. She certainly produces much industrial material, but she also sells her know-how, and many unseen services in insurance and overseas investment. These resources, visible and invisible, are her wealth, and the value of the pound sterling is backed up by the health of her economy. This is Hesed, and it must expand in order to continue the Lightning Flash down the Tree of Britain's prosperity. Should a slump set in and Britain not be able to fill the Hesed Sephira actively, a depression will follow, as the flow down the rest of the Tree diminishes. A quick glance at the paths will show where it will hit. Hesed, for obvious Cabalist reasons, must always be expansive, and here we observe the larger Tree of world trade. With the financial news always speaking of increasing gross national product we clearly sense the impulse of a vast global network of economies, each Hesed in each country contributing to the world's wealth, be it a natural resource, for instance of oil, or the highly technical skill of the aero industry.

In Hesedic terms on the spiritual Tree, this Sephira means the quality of Being, or the spiritual vitality present in a Religion or Philosophy. This may take the form of an expanding body of evolving people; saints, thinkers and men of action, of that Way. Such a phenomenon is seen in the Zohar period of the Cabala, in the Church and Scholasticism at the time of Thomas Aquinas, and in Islam during the great era of the Mevlevi Dervishes. Movements such as these are powerful in their influence, in that they reinforce the energy side of the Tree to balance with the Doctrine aspect of the Form Column. These Hesedic activities are also important because they contain the expanding impulse of the original teaching which is not only carried on over time, but is spread out from its space location. Any Religion or philosophy that does not move, or grow, dies; usually be-

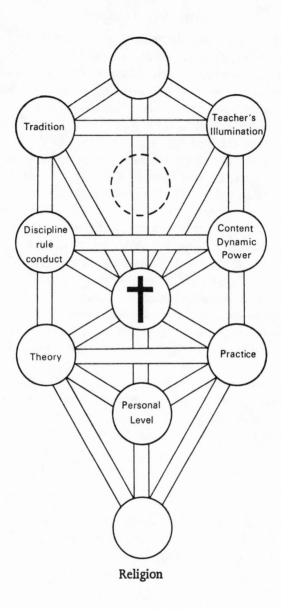

Religion

cause of the constraint of an over-active Binah, which creates a conservative Establishment who insist on preserving a teaching as a dogma. This inevitably discourages the Hesedic principle of taking in new and genuine converts, an absolutely necessary process if a Tradition is to survive. (The Zoroastrians face this one today.) Such numbers that a spiritual organism has contain the soul of a Church or School, and if there are no developing individuals present, the numbers may increase but the real, the Hesedic growth stops, though the body organisation might linger on for years. History is littered with dead and dying esoteric movements whose leaders did not realise that the growth point of their Tradition was not at the formal centre of their elect company but occurred more often in unscheduled meetings which flower when directly prompted by Hochma or Daat. Such graced gatherings, often unknown to the official hierarchy, are connected, at that moment in time, to the inner circle of that Tradition. As so often happens this phenomena is disagreeable to the Establishment who believe only they possess the Truth. The history of the Church bears witness in its initial rejection of many of its visionaries, like Tielhard de Chardin and St Teresa, and Orthodox Judaism had the same problem with Baal Shem Tov and Spinoza. Conventional Islam had to actually destroy Al Hallaj. Hesed is the dynamic of a spiritual Tradition. Standing below Wisdom, and receiving from Understanding and Knowledge, Hesed feeds down into Netzah and Tepheret, and across to Gevura. Hesed is the deep emotional reservoir of a Tradition, the powerhouse vital to its longevity and growth.

Gevura in spiritual terms is discipline. This is the focusing of the Hesed expansion. Without discipline the energy generated in Hesed would be lost. This application of the martial aspect of the Sephira is very marked in the monastic tradition with its strict rule and obedience, the latter directly related to the effect of Binah, the great Mother Church above. Discipline means to follow, though often an over-active interpretation is seen as a method of making the followers conform. While it is absolutely necessary for the love and power coming from Hesed to be controlled (or one has what is known as a stupid saint) this confining and channelling of religious emotion must not be fanatical. In extreme terms, when Gevura is the master and not the ser-vant, we have both the zealot and puritan operating under the jurisdiction of Binah's authority. Here is the Spanish Inquisition. The correct balance lies in the discipline being not for its own sake, but for the Tree as a whole.

In schools of philosophy Gevura is not only rule of con-duct, but the discipline of intellect. Here is good argument, intelligent discussion, and discrimination. Inspired visions are fine, but they must be sharply focused, or the meaning is diffused and lost. The power of discernment belongs here and is easily recognised in the Platonic dialogues. This is insight, well controlled and lucid in articulation with a razor-edged sense of true and false placed in the service of the highest cause.

In finance Gevura is the level of practical banking. It is here that the day-to-day adjustments are made: in the West, on Wall Street, the London Stock Exchange, and the Bourse in Paris. In each of these cities the banks perform (with their telex watchers on the various indexes) the fine balance of a house of cards. These cards are the delicate re-lationships of trust, the myriad transactions dealing in millions that flow back and forth. Here one industry blooms, there one fades. The price of steel rises, that of grain sinks. The dollar is steady, the pound rises, while the franc may be devalued and the mark revalued. Every moment is full of new possibilities. A country containing a huge reservoir of oil may have a revolution threatening the flow of energy and wealth from that area. Fast adjustments have to be made, quick decisions to switch to a stable area. The price rises. Capital, private or government, is released, or held in check, to maintain the market. Perhaps the price of gold, because of a political crisis, rises; so this useless but financial barometric metal is shifted from one vault to another. The buying and selling is fast and furious. In a falling market the atmosphere is frenetic, only a tight discipline and network of trusts holds a dangerous situation together. Even governments can be frightened by a series of bad decisions and panic selling. Only the over-riding governor of the country's treasury, the Bank of England for Britain, can check a bad run by altering the bank rate. This is Gevura at work in economics. Here is clean-cut decisiveness, based on hard facts and the mood of a market. It takes a military type of temperament to size up the day-to-day situation and take action that might well have to be reversed tomorrow. The apparent poker-face disposition of the financier is absolutely necessary. The best soldiers are the ones who never loose their cool.

Tepheret on the financial Tree is the particular system of that area or country. Thus we have the pound sterling area centred on London, to which are linked several countries not all in the British Commonwealth. Its face value is the pound, and what is seen on each bank note is the Queen of Britain's face. Here is the symbol of stability, tradition, a whole history of reliability stretching over what was the British Empire. The expression 'safe as the Bank of England' was no idle boast. It literally meant anyone carrying British currency, during Britain's primacy, could change it into the local money anywhere in the civilised world. This was because of the back-up of Britain's industry and military might. Here was an imperial economy, capitalist in outlook (the flag and trade went together), powerful and profitable. Most of the Empire's wars were fought over trade. The Anglo-French confrontation in the eighteenth century over India and North America is a prime example. On the other hand Tepheret can be a communist economy. Here the party, theoretically representing the people, takes charge of the finance of the country. Industry is nationalised and so is banking, but the same economic laws apply at Binah, though the profit goes to the state rather than the private investor. In the eastern block the image of the currency is much the same. The rouble rates just as much interest in the lives of Russians as the dollar does to Americans. True, the exchange between the two systems is not much, but this illustrates the point of Tepheret, that this Sephira is that particular currency and all it can purchase of the product of that community.

Tepheret, in religion or philosophy, is the face by which it is known. Be it church, mosque, or synagogue, the world sees it in its own image. Into Tepheret flow the paths of the Teacher, the tradition, the driving power, and the discipline, not to mention the direct flow through Daat from the crown of Kether. Here is the focus of a belief, as seen in the ritual. Be it the Mass, the reading of the Law, meditation, or the whirling of the dervishes, all express that tradition. Vast buildings bear witness to the body of each particular sect, their walls, roofs and floors speaking in stone of their theology, while the rites proclaim their persuasion. The Great Temple in Jerusalem, St Peter's in Rome, the Kaaba Shrine at Mecca, are more than mere physical settings for their religions. The Hebrew Temple, twice destroyed, drew the Jews back to Palestine after two millenia of exile.

From the viewpoint of philosophy a set of writings like the Cabalistic Zohar act as the Tepheret. The Tree of Life itself is a symbol, as well as a working diagram. The works of Plato have attracted thinkers down the ages, some of whom may never have read a word of his, but practise the platonic approach. The Islamic sufis have a collection of stories around which a whole teaching is focused. None of these objects, be they buildings or even Zen jokes, are it itself, yet all and every one relate to a particular philosophic system.

The invisible Sephira Daat, in the philosophical and religious context, might be likened to the spirit above such a movement. It is here that the Divine emanation comes directly into context. Perhaps this occurs during the Catholic Mass, or during the Cohen's blessing of the people in the Jewish high festivals, or during the ecstasy of the dervish turning—no one but the recipients can tell. This is indeed the point of transformation, when the Objective World enters the relative Universe.

In the realm of commerce Daat is knowledge. While the saint or philosopher may come to know about the sublime, the financial genius knows in his field about economics. Such a man though of mundane outlook might be a merchant banker, or even a prime minister like Benjamin Disraeli who bought the vital shares in the Suez canal company. It required a flash of vision to see the waterway as an important link in Britain's Far East trade, and a master's touch to move secretly and quickly, overriding more conventional buyers. This action proved a stroke of genius for Britain, who would have been at the height of her Empire, as she is now, at the mercy of whoever held the canal. Another seer at this level was the mediaeval Portuguese Prince, Henry the Navigator. He foresaw not just the new shipping lanes to be opened up, but the vast influx of Oriental and African wealth flowing back. Daat is an invisible Sephira—it is not consciously reachable unless certain prerequisites have been fulfilled on the economic Tree. That is why financial crises are common throughout the world. Real knowledge is comprehensive and objective, no chancellor of the Exchequer or government can be that disinterested, so we get a continuous shift from one Sephira to another on either side of the two outer pillars.

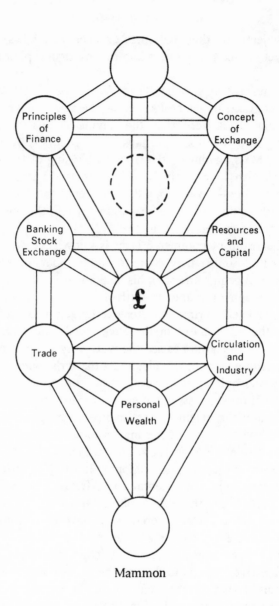

Mammon

In economic practice Netzah is the circulation of wealth It is also industry. It is here that raw materials are converted into goods, or effort into services. This is the most obvious part of the economic Tree. In every country the factories and their plant compose the vast muscles of industry, using up huge amounts of fuel. Here is the cycle of production, the endless chain of product and consumer. This is the autonomic system of a country slowly processing metals, minerals, natural materials, and recycled trash, into the national products that are to be used locally or exported. Into this cycle, flow imports; some in a crude state, others already refined. This flow includes sophisticated materials, tools, luxuries, all facilitated by the free interchange of money. A pound note may never leave the bank vault, but during a day's transaction it may have been lent to buy a boat of grain, then repaid in part of a debt on some nickel which is as yet still in the ground. The same note might change hands several hundred times in its (roughly) six-month life round the pockets, purses and tills of a country. This is the same as the blood system in a man, the coins as corpuscles, in a constantly circulating chain of wages and prices.

Netzah in philosophy or religion is practice. A man may be a Jew or a Christian by birth, but it may merely be nominal. The practising Moslem performs his daily obligations as part of his life. The devout Jew binds on his phylacteries without question, and no person professing to be a practising Christian would omit his prayers. There are of course degrees in all this. A man may merely pass through all the motions of religious practice. This was the problem of the Pharisees; to be seen to perform is not the same as actively performing and a devotee must refer to Hesed, the upper active Sephira, for real concurrence. Certainly a man may belong to a religion (his Tepheret) but this may be through pride of race, or tradition. This is not a real qualification. He must practise his religion as an integral part of his daily cycle, like eating and sleeping and all the processes of Netzah, before he is a really committed believer. For the philosopher, he too must practise. He must test everything he sees by his knowledge. To observe is not enough. He has to constantly relate his life to what he knows. There is no place for intellectual schizophrenia. He must act according to the principles he subscribes to. If he follows the Greeks he must be able to analyse. If he is a sufi he must constantly break habits. As a Jew he will constantly refer everything to the Torah, or the Tree. As one of the chief Jewish prayers says: 'no matter whether he is lying down or standing up, walking or eating'. This is the application of Netzah.

Hod is the theory of philosophy. It is also the reams of verbiage written down over the centuries on matters of religion. The Middle Ages up to the seventeenth century produced great numbers of books on theology, and wars were even fought over matters of doctrine. This is the Passive Form pillar playing an active role, with Gevura and Binah backing up Hod's theological precedents. In philosophy Hod is the Sephira where the subject is talked about. As the word 'about' suggests, it never actually deals with the experience, but comments on it. Netzah teaches it, the inner realm responds, but Hod, while knowing of it, can only (like this book) describe it in second- or third-hand terms. On the positive side Hod enables the man to be introduced to powerful ideas. With its outward-pointing orientation it can identify, taste and smell the echo of reality, though it always thinks, because it is the senses, it has the most direct contact with the real world. The ordinary logical mind and its memory bank is useful, but not an authority on such invisible subjects as philosophy and religion. It knows the line, verse and chapter, but not the meaning of the content, though it will claim it. It will however remind you of the volume containing the right quotation, or prompt you to meditate at the regular time. It will even inform you that something deep occurred inside your being, though it will not know what it is, however much it will try—and try it will.

Hod is trade on the economic Tree. As the mercurial ordinary mind and senses act as the go between in the inner and outer world, so Hod is the process of transaction in commerce. On the Bank of England pound note it says 'I promise to pay the bearer'. This is a word bond, no more than a printed offer which everyone trusts. Every day, over shop counters and a myriad other places where money changes hands, this promise is honoured. So much so, that even criminals trust it enough to want to steal large quantities of these bits of paper, a true mercurial action.

Hod is the point of communal interaction, the grass roots of economics. A great industry may be founded by millions in capital, but it is maintained by Everyman paying his electric bill, buying a car, or even going to the movies. The whole industrial effort is directed at everyman. The vast numbers of consumers lose sight of the fact that each one has in his or her purse the means to finance, not only the whole of industry, but the wealth and standing of a country. A nation may be large, but unless trade is fast and high it cannot afford the basics of life. These are financed from wages and taxes, every cent and penny adding to an immense river of money flowing throughout the system. The cheque book sidesteps the coin and note, but it is still Hod. The blank cheque is invalid until signed. With all the attributes of Mercury the whole basis of money at this level is verbal promise. This is the only way the financial system can work, for a producer, like a car worker, cannot use a spare wheel for his pay, nor can a servicer, like an insurance broker, eat his own policies, however vital to life he claims it to be.

Yesod on the financial Tree is the mass of the people and their standard of physical living. It is each person's personal wealth and how much he can earn in that particular economic system. He is not only the producer but the buyer of the produce of that Tree, and receives by the various paths the benefits of its industry and organisation. He can also receive its discrepancies, so that should a recession occur, he suffers the imbalance of each Sephira. The pound or dollar in his pocket is the Tepheret of his economic Tree and he sits directly underneath its aegis. It is also to be seen that Yesod forms part of a Hod and Netzah triad which describes the cycle of manufacturing, selling and buying, of which he is a vital link. The great financial crash of 1929 was partly because the masses could not afford to buy the goods they were making. If trouble, for instance civil disturbance, occurs in a community, this affects production and trade and therefore the people themselves. (Northern Ireland is a classic case.) A reverberating Tree is soon set up. If the stimulus disturbing the people is strong enough, like the injustice of land distribution, a revolution will be incurred that will bring about a change in the whole of the economic system. Yesod is the people, and each man's personal wealth. It is that people's ideal of values, be it a Rolls-Royce or a herd of goats.

Yesod in spiritual matters is the individual's level. A mass is composed of individuals, but unlike economics each man is more than a mere unit of production and consumption. He contains the whole Tree within himself. At Yesod he will reflect outwardly the face of a Jew or Moslem. Inwardly he may be in fact a great or gross man. This is his choice. He may choose to merely imitate his father, or even a master, acting as a reflection of his words and actions. The way his teacher smokes a cigarette can sometimes make a greater impression than what he is saying. His method of questioning may be copied without any understanding. Here is the persona, the bridge to learn, the barrier to imprison. The honest man who does not fulfil all the obligatory devotions may possess more wisdom than the keeper of the scrolls. The simple devotee, with no outward sign of learning, can

sometimes know more than the clever sage with his shim-
mering personality of other men's sayings. Yesod is the
reflection of all that has gone before. The lower paths focus
here. It is all that a man has acquired, though it will take
time for it to become really his own. Yesod is a reflection
of his philosophy or religion by the light he allows to shine
down from Tepheret. In Yesod he sees himself as if in a
mirror, until one day he sees that he can view directly from
Tepheret his own Essential Nature. Yesod is the moon and
its metal is silver. Tepheret is the sun and its metal is gold.
Herein lies the wealth of a man.

Malcut, for both finance and philosophy, is the kingdom
of the elements. For the financier it is the world of substance and energy out of which he builds his artifact kingdom. Constructing and destructing he moulds the planet's
surface, sometimes beautifully, sometimes badly. He works,
though he may not be aware of it, under the eye of a
great intelligence. He may tame Nature but he is never
her master. Man reaches out to the upper air and even the
moon, but he is still a child of the planet Earth and must
obey its laws. He can convert every stick and stone into a
new form but he will not make the volume of the earth
greater. He may release energy as he pleases, but it will be
no more than was there. Here is Malcut. The wealth of the
Earth is waiting to be refined, and though the financier,
industrialist, and worker may not realise it, they each con-
tribute more to the evolution of the planet than the pollution of it. A million years of man's presence have indeed
changed the face of the planet, and this is part of its natural
development in order to make it a more intelligent member
of the solar system. Through industry and technology men
have landed on the moon. Soon the biological spores of life
will be deposited permanently there. A second earth has been
begun; the Divine reaching down through man to create a
new kingdom—a Malcut root of a Lunar Tree of Life.

For the philosopher Malcut is his terrestrial body. This is his earth, his water, air, and fire. Here is his vehicle, his chariot pulled by the vital vegetable forces, with himself as the charioteer and sometimes as the deputy master. Malcut to the religious man is the temporary sojourn in the physical world. In this earthly shell he must reside, learning what lessons he can to refine his soul, until it drops from him, and returns back to the earth to be recycled via the worms into another growth. The Cabalist sees Malcut as the residue of Creation, the densest yet richest of materialities. In this apparently solid world he knows all the higher ones are hidden. Indeed they are fully present, every one interwoven or overlaid, and permeating through the Kingdom. Split an atom and Kether is there. Disect a cell and Kether is there. Look at a living man, deep within the densest bone and inside the most complex centre of the brain—Kether is there —and more. The Absolute is omnipotent.

XIV

Love Affair

The human race is a complete Tree of Life, with the male and female pillars demonstrating the relationship between the sexes. However, each person contains a complete Tree in miniature, with the elements of active and passive present in both men and women. In the action of courtship the interplay of the two great cosmic laws show themselves well in the unfolding of a mutual octave between two people drawn together by a third force. So here we will study one of mankind's favourite tales and observe, with our theory and practice, the phenomenon of Love.

Setting the party scene with an old song's romantic but often quite accurate description of the opening event, a man and a girl see each other across a crowded room. Beginning in Malcut, the hot smoky dimness was filled with jostling and dancing bodies. Talk and laughter abounded, and the air was pervaded with the smell of sweat and perfume. Our couple noticed each other quite early in the evening; the man initially attracted by the girl's fair hair, the girl by the intelligent strength of his face. They observed each other surreptitiously at first, their Hods gleaning information, not only by their senses, but in questioning the hostess and host about each other. The man found out her name, what she did and that she was unattached, while his Netzah aroused by the way she dressed provoked a Yesodic image of what might lie beneath. She reminded him of an old love and he could not help superimposing the memory on the girl, especially when he discovered their names were identical. The girl in her inquiry found that the man was unmarried, also that he was an architect. She was impressed for he not only had charm, but respectacle status. She suppressed the stupid idea that her parents would approve, as her Yesod placed him in the context of her home. Intrigued, she waited for him to approach as she instinctively acknowledged the signals of interest focused in her direction. The lower great physical triads of both their Trees were now tuned up for action.

The hostess quickly perceiving the situation introduced them and then left. With the goddess Venus only too present they both overlaid the mutual attraction with nervous small talk, each hiding behind their party personas. By his accent she discovered he was an American. By hers, he guessed she came from a middle-class English family. As their Hods discussed mutual acquaintances and friends both scrutinised each other. She liked the back of his neck and his voice. His eyes wandered over her body. She was also intelligent and well read. Just his type. She asked him about his work. He said he was in practice with three other young architects, and they were just beginning to make headway on their first big project of designing a school. She listened attentively, observing his hands and the liveliness of his eyes. She was very drawn to him. He was so different from the well-mannered fops she had been used to. His slightly battered looks quite aroused her.

Suddenly he said the noise of the party was unbearable. Would she like to slip out for some fresh air? To her own surprise she agreed without her usual obstruction to such a proposition. The party had become a bore, she rationalised, as they made their way through the dancers.

Walking down the street they were both strangely silent under the inner tension. He was reconsidering his standard method by which he got girls into bed. It was somehow inapplicable, for there was an unnerving element present in the sense of already knowing what would happen, though why he should think this he could not fathom. She was confused. Normally she did not allow herself to be so easily isolated from a party where she had been safe with her friends. Here she was with a complete unknown. Or was she? The question was odd for she felt she had met him before, though where she could not tell.

He began, English style, to talk about the weather, and soon they were comparing their respective countries' climates and seasonal conditions in the cities of New York and London. All through this pointless conversation there was another, a Hod, Netzah, Yesod, and Malcut dialogue going on. It was in the touch of his hand on her arm, and her response in the question and answer game of the sexes. The tension increased as they approached her small flat. She wanted to invite him in but her judgement (Gevura) said no. It was too early in the evening and too soon. Her upbringing and her image of herself would not allow it, she told herself. He, detecting her hesitance, did not press her, and suggested they walk on. She was relieved and moved by this sensitive response to her resistance. Maybe, she thought as they passed her front door, she would not object to being seduced. Suddenly energy that came from she knew not where flowed through her limbs, and taking his offered hand she accepted and gave the first kiss. From that moment on they were both in another realm. (the Animal triad). Abruptly there was no darkness. The moon emerged as if from nowhere, and the stars appeared to be twice as bright in a deep vast sky. Everything about them, even the buildings, seemed alive and full of colour. They saw, as they walked arms about each other, with such clarity, heard and smelt with such acuteness, that every street was filled with an extraordinary magic. With both functional sides of the Tree excited, the triad of self-consciousness was stimulated.

They wandered for miles, and talked the hours away. By two in the morning they had covered each other's entire personal history, and knew all there was to know in words. At his front door she assented to the suggestion that she would like a coffee before going home. As they climbed the stair in a dreamlike haze, the air became charged with passion.

The coffee was made but not drunk. A deeper hunger had taken command. Gradually undressing, each explored the other's body, not only for pleasure but in an unconscious instinctive probing to see that every part was normal. Naked, they enjoyed all their senses, each touch, smell and taste adding to the inner heightening of bodily sensations and feelings. In bed, close in embrace, their minds fluctuated between passing thought and complete silence : Hod, Netzah, and Malcut. There was little talk, the only communication being touch, sight, and sound. Yesodic dreams continually clouded their brains, separating them, as romanticised imagery was projected onto the physical reality. His eye observed faults in her beauty, but this was overlaid. She discerned flaws in his confidence, these however were ignored, washed away in the gentle passion she sensed building up within her body. Last night she had been alone and frustrated. Now she was elated, almost on the edge of release. Slowly the man drew her closer together, until their rhythms coincided. Nearer they approached, blending into single motion. Suddenly they were one and in the climax of ecstasy they met and dissolved into nothing, as they rose up the column of equilibrium from Tepheret to Daat. And Adam knew Eve.

Slowly out of the ecstatic void they emerged, separated, to become individuals, as gently they returned to their bodies again. Cloudy thoughts and feelings ebbed back, but they could not drown the profound meeting they had experienced. Nothing could erase, not even the body's reverberat-

ing fatigue, that momentary yet timeless contact. Only that
seemed real. They looked at each other in the dim light,
seeing only a smiling face of skin and bone. True, the eyes
still retained the consciousness, but where was the person
each had contacted, face to face? He touched her cheek,
and this was reassuring to both of them. From that point
on, moment by moment, they descended into the world of
ordinary living. In her, practical thoughts began to test
romanticism. She had been caught once before by infatua-
tion. And yet it was not the same. This was permeated
through with a curious sense of knowing, of recognition.
She sighed, exhausted in her pleasant fatigue. Never before
had she felt so safe, even in the most familiar surroundings
of her home.

He, in the limp ebb tide of his passion, lay thinking. This
experience could only be matched by his first love of long
ago on his uncle's New England farm. Without the smell of
hay, or larks overhead in the summer sky, he had relived
one of the most moving experiences of his life. This was
remarkable because he had had love affairs and all, in the
light of this night, were shown up as mostly physical.
it was a shock. He had not really known any of them.
This girl was the first he had really seen as more than a
woman.

They both lay silent for a long time, wondering what had
happened. Here was no casual night passage. Something important had occurred. They had been joined for a brief instant and neither could ever forget that moment. Whatever
happened in the relationship that was to follow, nothing
could ever break this connection. Tepheret had met
Tepheret.

By morning, however, enchantment had set in. The hard
light of dawn and ordinary life called on sentiment, and they
constructed a romantic idyll to preserve the feeling of the
night. Soon the original contact was lost as they sank into

the self-enchanting games lovers play. Yesod had re-established itself.

Over the ensuing weeks the idyll bore them on exotic wings, changing every place and time they met into a fairy-land. Affection grew in shared experience, and gradually as the honeymoon phase faded a quite genuine love between them was generated. But something new began to appear with the raising of Gevura. Mutual criticism began to emerge. At first silent, it developed into occasional irritation as each began to examine the image each had imposed on the other. This led on to comment, then bickering when they saw their idol dissolve into human weakness. At times there was open quarrelling when one refused to conform to the other's dream. He found her possessive and demanding and she discovered he was extremely moody. Occasionally exchanges were sharp and belligerent, only to be dissolved on the bed of Venus where Mars was placated.

By the sixth month of their relationship they reached a turning point. The tinsel novelty had gone, but they felt strongly enough about each other to consider living together. This had precipitated an unexpected crisis. While they agreed that running two flats and one love affair was inconvenient, both also shared the view of remaining independent. In this lay the rub. Such trial marriages were not uncommon in their circle, but there was also the question of property and territory which revealed a crucial issue. When it came to signing the lease for the apartment whose place would it be? Each discovered a strong sense of ego. Neither of their Yesods would step down to be the tenant partner. Both wished to be the retaining landlord, should they eventually split up. Each saw themselves as sacrificing their integrity for the convenience of the other. A row actually developed outside the estate office. He felt his masculinity insulted, she her security threatened. Maybe they had better part now, they concluded. They were obviously both completely selfish and totally incompatible.

That night in bed, after a miserable evening in her place, the miraculous happened again. At the climax of making love, now a pleasurable routine, the Tepheret connection made on their first night was re-established. Suddenly they were one again. Perhaps only for a second, but long enough to see there was a deep bond between them. Here Hesed was touched upon. Abruptly, all the conflicts became trivial in the radiance of this expansive inner emotion. Everything suddenly was forgiven, and all real or imagined hurts were forgotten. Their egos retreated, became magnanimous, each allowing the other to exist in its own right. They saw their relationship could go on but with each person developing separately.

Time tested their relationship, and they gradually grew to respect and understand one another as the faculties of Binah slowly came into operation. They had their periods of difficulty, particularly when she saw friends have children, or his work went through a bad period. Occasionally even their intimacy became stale, and they indeed argued like a married couple, each knowing by now the other's habits and attitudes. Their second major crisis came when they realised they could go no further. They must change the half-completed relationship or separate. Neither wished to move, and so they both embarked on a series of disastrous love affairs elsewhere.

Within two months they had returned to each other, both recognising in the pain of their experiences that they much preferred each other. This was seen in a flash one night, as their reunion not only reminded them of all they had shared but showed them, by the past pattern, all that was possible for the future. Here Binah connected with Hochma, illuminated the obvious fact they were designed for each other, foibles and all. Daat completed the self-evident realisation with its extraordinary certainty, and they decided they had no other choice but to marry. The Tree of their relationship was all but finished.

At the wedding a curious event occurred. When the minister carried out the ceremony both the man and the girl perceived, during the rite, a subtle joining within them. It was as if something from above confirmed their union. Moreover, as the bride turned to the groom she suddenly knew that on first sight she had unconsciously recognised her husband.

Our story is perhaps a classic situation, for it contains the principle of mutual growth and balance in the respective Trees of each partner. It also demonstrates the cabalistic tradition related to men and women wherein the intimate connection is a direct analogue of the Tree, and the meeting of Heaven and Earth. Marriage, a real union and not merely a legal arrangement, is rare because in most people one or more Sephiroth are not working correctly. An active Gevura is a common reason for shrewish wives, and an unbalanced Netzah-Hod relationship has wrecked many marriages, while a masking Yesod of lies has outwardly preserved more than one marital disaster.

Sex, quite contrary to a puritan or permissive outlook, is indeed not meant to be misused, but it has to be related to a cosmic not a custom situation. At the climax of the act in a harmonious and full relationship many things are possible, and it is not without reason it is called occasionally the poor man's meditation. Here is the meeting of two Trees; the merging of twin identities who loosen for a moment, through their bodies, the bonds of Earthly existence. The nearest thing to mystical experience for most men, it allows them to glimpse, with their Eve, through the gates of Eden into Paradise. In this context marriages are indeed made in Heaven, the Bride of Malcut awaiting the Bridegroom of Kether, with Jacob at Tepheret and Rachel at Yesod, held between Heaven and Earth.

XV

Birth-Life-Death

Continuing the story from the last chapter we examine two
Trees resulting from the conception of a child. The first
concerned with its gestation and birth; the second with its
subsequent process on entering the world outside the womb,
with its growth and death. Here we study descending and
ascending octaves.

Our couple now married decide to have a child; or Fate,
whatever this strange element might be, places them in a
situation where a child is conceived. Seen from the point
of view of the Tree Hochma is the Father and Binah is the
Mother, and when they come together, united in Yesod, and
if the conditions are right, that is, that the Column of
Equilibrium is charged with creation, conception occurs in
Daat. From the father comes the active principle, all the
male attributes of him, his family and race. From Binah the
same contributions are made with the feminine elements
added. Here the dynamic is formulated, the history of two
lines of generation woven in the dance of the chromosomes.
The sex of the child is probably determined in Binah, as is its
dark or light hair, tendency to grow tall or small, and have
a weak or strong chest. If we suppose the father is Jewish and
the mother English we get a blend of the ethnic characteristics which in life will give the child an insight and understanding of two outlooks. He may be volatile and practical,
or phlegmatic yet shrewd. Dozens of combinations are
possible on this level. In Binah also is the probable setting of

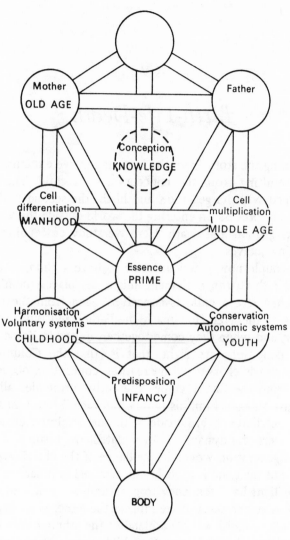

Birth-life-death

all the clocks, both biological and spiritual, as well as the general temperament.

After conception the Lightning Flash passes on to Hesed. Here begins the process of organic expansion and growth. Within a matter of days the fertilised ovum has divided into a number of cells and formed into a hollow ball. This mass continues to expand at an extraordinary rate, until, fed by nutriment obtained from the wall of the mother's womb, it has become an embryonic disc. At this point the Gevura principle at work in gestation begins with the differentiation of the cells into various functions, the chief of which is the formation into specialist roles of three cell layers. These are the entoderm, which becomes the inmost systems of digestion and its associated functions; the mesoderm, which produces the middle zone of muscles, bones and connective tissue; and the ectoderm, which forms eventually into the outer skin, the brain and spinal column. The Gevura differentiation takes place when the embryonic disc is still less than an eighth of an inch in diameter.

From this time on Hesed and Gevura work together, Hesed producing growth, Gevura defining and determining organs and functions. In the ectoderm the head begins to form, the nervous system is laid out and the lenses of the eyes are resolved. For the mesoderm the different muscles and bones are focused, with the lungs, alimentary canal, sex and blood rapidly evolving; while the entoderm lines the breathing passage, alimentary canal and bladder. This interbalanced labour goes on in correct sequence governed by the plan in Binah, and generated by the creative impulse begun in Hochma.

Tepheret announces the presence of the Essential Nature. By its position on the Lightning Flash it would imply that when the embryo is whole, the particular intelligence imbued by the central Column of Consciousness, headed by Kether, and focus of the four previous Sephiroth, arrives.

Here it waits, during the period of gestation, for birth; though in the case of miscarriage or abortion it may, as the Hebrew prayer book says, 'pass by the world without entering it'.

The gestation process continues with Netzah not only setting all the biological rhythms and cycles of blood, digestion etc. in motion, but also in installing the principle of conservation, so that there is a continuous renewal, be it of cells, the instinct of self-preservation, or of regeneration of the species in the desire for sex. This Netzah principle applies right through, not only in the organism but in the person's psyche, which continually seeks conducive habits that preserve his sense of wellbeing. While the embryo is still connected to the mother and participates in her circulation, its desire to survive is very present, and communicates itself through the Netzah in the mother, whose lethargic state is designed to obviate any personal erratic behaviour. She is under the rulership of Venus and the Moon, the twin godmothers of Nature.

Hod might be called here the harmonising principle. Not only are various sensory organs completed by the Hodian nervous systems, but the whole organism is tuned within the limiting defines of Gevura into a highly responsive instrument. Hod permeates the embryo, passing data back and forth so that the preceding processes are brought into fine adjustment. To illustrate its function in a negative way : when a group of cells is not in sympathy with the tuning of the organism as a whole, cancer may occur, and an unbalanced Netzah will supply it with nutriment and maintain the malignant growth. Unless Gevura is informed and all the data passed on to the related Sephiroth, the tumour will expand and destroy its benefactor body, and subsequently itself, so selfish is its orientation. Hod makes it possible for the body to perceive what is going on. By its ability to scan, it can learn of the slightest abberation, then inform Netzah, for example, to send out white blood corpuscles to counter infection in the system. Acting as the balance to Netzah, Hod also looks outwards through the senses to monitor the environment. This is even at work in the womb when the child kicks until it finds itself a more comfortable position.

Yesod in this case is the personality of the whole organism, as yet unimpressed by the outside world. It sits in the middle of the Hod, Netzah, Malcut triad, the modelled but smooth wax of the brain, body, and psyche of the child. Like a mirror it is made in a certain way, perhaps clear, maybe misty, even distorted, depending on what occurred before during gestation. It carries no memories, only built-in characteristics, flaws and foibles. A family gift for music is perhaps latent, or a tendency to violence; maybe also an aptitude for mechanics, or an inherent dislike for high places. Not active, these things, created by a combination of the particular balance of the Sephiroth, may lie dormant throughout life, until brought out by stress or some conducive circumstance. A Mozart in a mining village would perhaps never get beyond the chapel organ, while a mechanical genius could well be wasting his time playing in the London Philharmonic Orchestra, never having time in the rush of a professional musician's life to take up his hobby of inventing gadgets. Yesod might loosely be called the mind, the ordinary mind, and we shall explore it further when we take the Tree in the opposite direction from birth to death.

Malcut, the Kingdom of the Elements, is the physical body. All the other Sephiroth supply the energy and form which creates the physical organism we see emerging from the womb. From Yesod upwards there are principles, like the desire for survival. They are manifest through the body, but it itself is merely a vehicle, an ever-changing aggregate of cells of which only the brain tissue has anything approaching the length of life of the man himself, for many cells last merely a day or so, others at most a few weeks. We are a continually changing standing wave, as science calls such a phenomenon. The only apparently permanent elements are the workings of the Sephiroth which maintain our consciousness, form, and energy, while increasing the body's size up to maturity, before the exhausted organism, no longer capable of supporting cellular life, collapses at death. It is interesting to repeat from Genesis the idea that we have fallen or descended into coats of skins, that we are bound by the laws of organic life, denied for a period the upper garden of Eden. On conception we are imprisoned in a physical form, and then ejected from the womb of Eve into the natural kingdom from where we begin on birth the octave of return via death.

On birth we take our first breath. With this sudden jolt a child is severed from its mother at the end of a creative octave and becomes an independent being. Anyone witnessing a birth knows the sense of profound impact not only on them, but particularly on the babe, which reacts in a definite way to its entry into our dimension. Some arrivals do not wish to embark on the journey and are stillborn, others prefer to hold back until they are dragged in by a slap on the back. Others fight the shock of being removed from the protection of the womb, while yet others accept they are here, at least for a while. This initial period is sometimes called the 'Age of Wisdom'—a curious name more suited to the end of life, yet from another view birth and death are the same place. Therefore this name may well be valid. However, no babe as yet has the vocabulary to explain its experience, but then this is equally true of mystics just emerging from ecstasy, so we are left with the wondrous impression of the babe's awakening into our World, followed by its Hod-Netzah yell for warmth and food as the two side pillars of function come into full independent action.

Malcut is the shrivelled wet and living body of the baby. From this moment on it begins its journey back to Kether containing the whole Tree, as Kether is in Malcut, but this Tree will not perhaps be seen outwardly, except over the years as the person grows back up it again. The first stage is the path between Malcut and Yesod—babyhood. In this period not only is the body rapidly increasing its volume, but it is also soaking up internal and external information. From Hod it absorbs through its senses the smells, sounds, tastes, and sights of its mother. Touch is perhaps the most important sensor, with temperature and comfort playing an important part in forming a contribution to its world image in Yesod. Netzah adds to the picture, the baby slowly recognising the daily rhythm and response of the parent who comes running to its every call. Later, as the Yesodic image is extended beyond intimate bodily exploration and reaction to internal cycles, the baby begins to push out its sensory field, throwing things from its bed as part of the programme for studying height and distance. By the beginning of childhood (each Sephiric stage blends into the next) the baby has begun to control its functions, walk and speak; all the faculties of physical Hod.

The period of Hod is the time when the child learns about everything around it. Always curious it questions and explores continuously the local geography of its home, and the intellectual world opened up by reading and the media. Boyhood is occupied with experimentation, ranging from seeing how much weight a tree branch can take, to simple chemistry. Museums are a favourite place, and so are any holes or caves. Vast collections of fascinating junk are accumulated, and an endless inquiry into the biggest, strongest, longest, and heaviest things and creatures on the earth are conducted. This surely is the Sephira of Mercury with its chameleon range of interests, including tricks, deception, and even thievery—as any orchard owner knows! Speed and lightness are all important, and the agility displayed in the school playground is self evident, as is the cacophony of young, high-pitched, mercurial voices. As adolescence approaches the child has a very clear world picture. Its persona is now well formed, its education covering over its Essential Nature, sometimes so much so, that it blocks out the light. This is well demonstrated by the English public school system which can overlay a boy's true nature with such a strongly conventional social mask, that often it imprisons him for life. Admirable as a tool in service to a man's real self, the persona is a bad master if there is to be any real development. As frequently observed, many people do not free themselves beyond Yesod and Hod, preferring to eat, drink, and talk in old clichés and habits picked up at school. In life their values are governed by gratification or impressionability, their desires often directed by people who have the determination of Gevura, the power of Tepheret, or the desire of Netzah. This may appear somewhat scathing, but the western world in particular runs its commerce on the evocation of these weaknesses and dominances.

Youth is the time of Netzah. With it comes the awareness of beauty and love. Girls grow conscious of their bodies, and boys of the rising of passion. It is the age of Venus, a time to wear the latest becoming style, know the current musical hit, pass through all the sweet intrigues of romance in a pleasant world of poetry. This is the time of flower children and endless unexpected pregnancies. Here is a dreamer's realm, recognisable in *Romeo and Juliet*, and *West Side Story*. Energy and ease, ebb and flow; courtship passes through the cycle of seduction, orgasm, and relaxation. Here is Netzah or Eternity, with the continuous round of love passing from partner to partner in a long chain of embraces. The world is rosy. Youth has no sorrows other than that of unrequited affection, and there is always another beloved to fill that heartache. Pain, illness, and death have no place here, everyone is vital and beautiful without a trace of rheumatism. To sleep out of doors is fun, to sing to the guitar till dawn no physical problem. Fatigue is quickly washed away by love, and the body's waxing strength can take any punishment. This is the age when the boy and the girl separate from home, the intimacy of love projecting them into the first sense of independence. This is the spring before the full flowering of a man or woman.

Tepheret is the prime of Life. At this point Nature has reached her zenith. She has endowed all that organic Life can impart, and the Essential Nature has at its command all the physical equipment it might need. Many great works of art are created during this age (Tolstoy was in his mid-thirties when he wrote *War and Peace*), and men often come into their own at this time if they have progressed beyond Netzah. Those who have not, still amuse themselves with love affairs and pleasures far beyond their years, hoping to retain a youth since gone. Modern advertising exploits this, convincing the mature that the physical qualities of youth have more to offer than the intelligence of their own experience. Men and women who are bodily orientated forget the possibilities of their souls and strive to remain young till even the most expensive cosmetics cannot defend the illusion of eternal beauty and vitality. Organic time cannot be frozen.

The age of Tepheret is unique, because lying on the central axis of consciousness it opens access to inner development. While Yesod supplies awareness of the outer world, and Hod and Netzah perform their functions, Tepheret opens the gate to immortality. Through the true self-consciousness of a man, with a fully operative and well-running machine, it is possible for him to see, at this physical peak, the nature of his whole life. At this point he can know where his career lies, can foresee a direction to be taken. Called traditionally the 'Judgement Seat', Tepheret enables him to decide at the mid-point of his life whether he chooses, or is made to choose. Here a man has the power to be himself. He may be a servant of a large company but he can be himself, have his own integrity, individuality. Certainly the temptation of ego is present, but this at least indicates a man has matured and the remedy is inherent. A real devil has more possibility of growth than a shadow of a man who lives through only his Yesod, which is sometimes no more than a collection of imitations acquired, borrowed and stolen from other men.

Gevura is the period of determination. It could be called manhood, that is, when the power of the full stature is applied to a direction. Taking the symbol of Mars we can see the hallmark of a man who has reached this level and age. He could be a company director, or an artist working along his own original line. There is courage present and discrimination. He does not deviate, except to adjust to problems that are probably more learning situations than fences to be jumped en route to his ambition. There is an emotional element in his work. He continues to labour just for interest, where lesser men only work for money. Something drives him. It may be that he wants a better home, or to give his children a good education. Whatever it is, it gives him a surety and a decisiveness that marks him out. Negatively it can make him aggressive, the ruthless careerist who will tread on anybody who gets in his way. His motivation may be ego, as the Hod-Tepheret-Gevura triad, untempered by a strong balancing Hesed-Netzah-Tepheret triad, drives him on. Conversely, he can with this level of judgement discriminate finely, have an eye for situations, products and people that makes employers want him as their servant. Such a man is invaluable in a negotiating team as an expert, and this again will single him out as a man with a definite skill and knowledge that is his very own. Manhood is reached by few men as real masters, though some are forced to superficially act the part in order to compete and dominate. This is external pressure and not true to a person's inner nature. In time such a man wonders whether it was worth the effort when younger men replace him. When our man reaches the point where he goes it alone, takes a decision, perhaps against advice or even common sense, to follow his own star, we can say he has reached the Gevura initiation.

The period of Hesed is middle age. This is perhaps after the tough long haul of bringing up a family, or that part of a career which separates the professional from the amateur. By this time a man has a wealth of experience, maybe the material goods too, that go with this age. He possesses most of the things he desired—perhaps success, personal satisfaction, even outworn delusion. He has reached a point where the pressure can be alleviated. He is more tolerant, more benign. Certainly he works hard, but not with the same verve. This is not only because his physical powers are beginning to wane, but because with his expanded view he can see the best way to accomplish an operation. He sees that rapid action and determination have their place, and that younger men can fulfil this better than he can, but he also sees the overspill of a scheme, the ramifications he could not know when he was a single-minded man. Life becomes more pleasant, work is important, but he can afford to relax, be generous. He is, if the desire to work is still strong, more inclined to look at his industry on a grander scale. Money or status is no longer the consideration. There is a certain joy in what he does. He may even become suddenly benevolent and socially conscience-stricken, want to help the poor as the American millionaire Peabody did; even start philanthropic foundations, like Ford and Rockefeller. If he is a loner, perhaps an artist, and he has really matured far beyond the Gevura competitive age, he may wish to help younger painters or writers as T. S. Eliot did. This is indeed the age of the Jovial, as the Martial was of the Gevura period.

Between Hesed and Binah lies the invisible Sephira of Daat. This is the point in a man's life when he really knows what it has all been about. If he has evolved this far—and most people do not because they prefer to remain in the illusion of their most pleasant time, usually their youth— an evolved man will relate all he has learnt to the pattern of his life. From this position directly above Tepheret he will be able to look back and see with knowing eyes all the winding paths he trod. This will lead him to a deep realisation that life is a game in which the art is to participate, but not be caught. The world is a literal stage, and a man's life is a walk-on part. He will recognise this and observe with cynicism or humour, depending on how he arrived at the view, that there is a second birth to undergo before death. In many who reach this conclusion, the void of Daat, or the disappearance of the ego, may be too much. In death they know they must give up all their worldly gains, but they hold on, clinging to memories and possessions, avoiding the second great shock and potential birth since they entered the world. Those who see this point as an opportunity begin to retire from the world before they are forced to vacate it by death. They may continue to work in the world, but their attitude is not of it. In the Indian tradition a householder hands over to his sons all his worldly duties and retires. In the West a man may do the same but join a golf club. However, even in the technological societies of Europe and North America there are some who follow the same idea of spiritual retirement, and it is important to remember that a person can arrive at this point at any time. Many a remarkable man has made his fortune before forty and devoted the rest of his life to personal evolution, be it joining a monastery or, like Schliemann the German millionaire, devoting it to archaeology. This critical change brings us to Binah.

Binah is old age. Contrary to the usual belief that this period is a terminal one of running down, it is the preparation for the dynamic of birth of death. Certainly the body is decaying and all the vital processes are sluggish, but the invisible part of man that inhabits this physical shell is, or should be, full of a lifetime's experience. While the body can no longer run a mile, usually an unnecessary accomplishment in old age, the soul can ponder on the material collected over the years. Silence and stillness are all that are needed. A good head and heart, backed up by a slowly clearing memory of earlier times so characteristic of old age, can review life, and come to an understanding not possible in a busy outward existence. Time is the quality of Binah, whose traditional planet is Saturn. Here is the ability to survey decades, see the links and knots of years, use the knowledge of Daat to unravel mysteries of fate in hindsight, see how certain meetings and partings were fatal, perceive that particular situations taught precisely the needed lesson. A whole library of intimate films can be replayed without the pressing desires, value judgement, or over-indulgent assessments. Scenes can be relived with greater clarity, the true facts about situations learned years later, piecing together the unknown. Here at Binah in the winter of physical life is the possibility of sensing the next spring. Laid out is a whole life-year with all its seasons. In the closing in of the senses the inner world becomes more real, the invisible realm closer. Childhood memories return, smells and sights recalled that were long forgotten. Old faces, even the dead, constantly visit the contemplator and behind them are intimations of paradise. To the unthinking this appears to be the point of departure, to the thoughtful it is an approaching. Here is the leap across the Tree to the Hochma. Those who reach old age and are still spiritually undeveloped see the reversed jump of the Lightning Flash as the blinding light of obliterating death. To those who have understood the meaning of their lives through Binah and Daat, death is perceived quite differently. They glimpse through the curtain of Hochma a bright world beyond. In the silent, deep thought of the inner intellect, illumination comes not to frighten, as death does the unprepared, but to illuminate the path back to Kether—the Crown. In Hochma is the wisdom of a lifetime flashing down the years through all the Sephiroth to Malcut. As death separates the soul of a man from his coat of skin, and draws him up into the next world, those present at his death will recognise that a cosmic event has taken place. Indeed so potent is this occurrence that its impact is felt often over a great distance and for many years. This is the power of Hochma, in death as profound an insight as for those who witness a birth.

In Kether is the end and the beginning. It is the open Crown through which the spirit enters and departs, sometimes to come and at others to return.

XVI

Time

Having looked at birth and death, let us use the Tree in a quite different way to examine Time. First we must realise that there are different orders of Time. The method of using a clock, be it a twenty-four-hour or a microsecond meter, is more convenient than accurate. The Sun, for instance, for most of the year arrives at the noon meridian early or late, and the time, according to the stars, has to be continually adjusted to make a scientific constant. So we must leave the common understanding of time alone.

The most familiar form of Time we know—that is for human beings, for every creature has its own measure—is what is called Passing Time. This is seen on the screen of Yesod, which views the world of Malcut as a passing show, a continuous stream of images focusing and dissolving in between the inner daydreams. At night, when the path between Yesod and Malcut is shut down, the daydreams come to the forefront like stars at night, and Time appears to do strange things. This Passing Time is the one we generally regard as real and correlate to the clock. This is an illusion and quite unreliable, as the contrast between a boring or an interesting day will tell you, by the way the hours drag in one, and go too swiftly in the other. It is apparent from a little thought and observation that the clock measures nothing of our personal life, though it is useful for arranging meetings and other external practical matters. As for our real sense of time our watch is useless. The young man waiting for his girl finds ten minutes intolerably long and the parting kiss

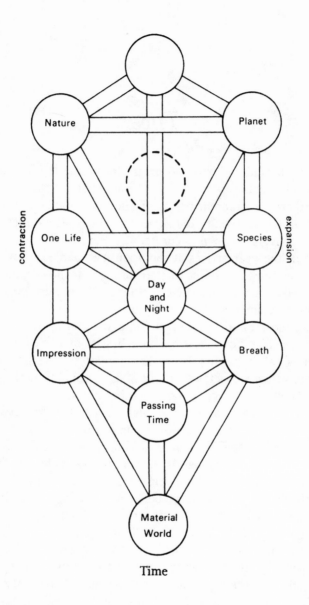

Time

unbearably short for quite different subjective reasons. This is the result of the interaction of different levels and dimensions of Time.

Man is a Tree of Life and each Sephira has its own time scale. If we take Tepheret as a day and night, the essence of Time, we see a complete cycle around which the various clocks of the Tree function. In Tepheret is a conscious measure. A man can take in a whole day, his being can perceive it as one piece. Time in the other Sephiroth is either too long or too short to grasp in entirety, but a day is comprehensible by his body and soul.

Normally a man sees the world through Yesodic time. He views the passage of events imagining them to be real, but when he suddenly wakes up, perhaps in the middle of a car accident, everything changes. Often the most memorable characteristic of such an event is that time appears to slow down. Perhaps while out driving a pedestrian slips in front of him. He catches sight of the fall and sees the whole action quite clearly in a fraction of a clock second, yet he takes in more in that instant than he saw in a whole day of Yesodic time. He swerves, brakes his car and watches it apparently drift slowly into collision with a lamp post. His body, however, working on another time scale, cannot respond fast enough to correct the skid. It seems to be extraordinarily sluggish even though he knows his reflexes are incredibly fast. He observes the situation unfold gradually before his eyes, the curiously impartial watcher within himself suddenly alerted. He follows the action as if he were viewing a slowed-down film frame by frame. Some sportsmen know this phenomenon well, and see a cricket or baseball approach them more like a slow-moving balloon than an express train. This is the Hod view of Time which sees Time in infinitesimal impressions or reverberations. They can be as short as a one ten-thousandth of a second. One of these impressions can freeze a tiny event into a readable picture for the mind. Our memories are full of such instances. Nor should it be rare, for our nervous and sensory systems are based on this high-frequency response. Hod's highest range of frequency is our shortest impression, or one fine electric spark in length. Looking through Hod's time scale a minute is made up of thousands of such flashes. If it were not so the eye could not function, though to our normal sensibility these ever-changing images blend into the continuous flow called sight.

It is possible to heighten our sensibility so as to appear to slow down Hod's time at will. This can be done unnaturally with drugs like LSD, but not only is this unlawful in a spiritual sense, it is as dangerous as putting rocket fuel in a small car. It will go fast for a while, then burn it out—for ever. The lawful way is to acquire this consciousness by intelligent and diligent cultivation. The Arts are one means of attaining it, as many painters demonstrate with their frozen moments on canvas and many composers attempt to evoke such an acute state with their music. The cinema recognises the dramatic impact of slowing time down. For those who practise a spiritual discipline this phenomena is familiar. Here is one of the gates to higher consciousness. In the alert state that comes with, for instance, a meditation practice, a nod or a single word can convey a whole statement in an instant. Only a sharp and well-tuned Hod could catch such a conversation. Perhaps a story will illustrate this dimension: An angel once appeared to a man one night. Naturally he was rather surprised and knocked over a jug. This was instantly forgotten as he was carried up through all the levels of the Heavenly Kingdom to the Foot of God Himself. After seeing all the celestial sights he was brought down through the worlds and eventually returned to his bed, just in time to observe the jug he had knocked over hit the floor.

Netzah is a breath, that is, one complete cycle relating to

the inner and outer world. The body is full of clocks each with its own rhythm, the chief being the heart beat, but this does not directly connect with the world outside. A breath does, and in its rhythm it partakes of both exterior and interior. This gives it a unique view, for it reveals a corresponsive relationship. A moment of fright demonstrates this reciprocal reaction. Throughout a breath, in such a moment, the whole situation is taken in by the thousands of impressions flooding into the Hod faculty. By the end of that same breath they have been analysed and the Netzah autonomic system has adjusted the organism for flight or fight.

Anyone under the spell of love knows the moment to moment changes in mood and metabolism. The relationship is measured out in breaths, long or short, and the sequence extends like an ecstatic chain to the climax breath of orgasm. This link with the instinctive mind connects with Nature, and sometimes a beautiful view literally takes the breath away. Here is an inherent response, and it can be observed to act in sympathy at the turn of the evening, or at dawn in a forest, when the vegetable world reverses its oxygen-carbon dioxide respiration. At such a moment there is a distinct pause, as the systole and diastole of Nature changes over. Netzah is the clock of breath measuring out not the instant of Hod, but complete moments. These are not just impressions but a whole situation, be it a vast landscape or a first embrace.

Tepheret is the essence of Time. For man it is the cycle of the Sun through a day and night. For a mayfly, a creature whose existence is but a few hours, a day is a whole life. To the biosphere a year, the complete round of seasons, is maybe a day. To the Earth, a day is perhaps many decades, one rotation on its own axis merely being its shortest registerable impression; and for the Sun, the radiation ebb and flow as measured in the Earth's tropical to ice-age cycle may be just a breath. Tepheret is the slide plate of our cosmic microscope and whatever we put there, in this particular examination, will be the day and night for that entity. For us, we can see quite plainly that we live by the beat of activity and rest. One twenty-four-hour cycle is a mirror of our life. Our awakening is birth, our morning growth, noon is prime, afternoon our wane and evening our retirement, with death's stepbrother sleep completing the circle. True, not all our dawns coincide with the clock on the wall, some of us begin to wake up at midday and others after midnight. Everyone has his or her own setting or personal chronology for the day, but without exception everybody has to obey the ebb and flow of the cycle. The vital forces can be drawn upon to extend their period, but to drain these emergency reservoirs is to eventually court death, for it is contrary to the mainspring of life which drives our personal clock.

Gevura is a single life. In man it is connected with the emotional aspect of his being. It is the feeling of a life. Sometimes great portrait painters use this faculty to catch in their pictures the whole of a man's existence. A Rembrandt is more than a remarkable likeness. It is layer upon layer of impression, moments, and Essential Nature. It is the sum total of a demeanour, attitudes, and deeds. In the portraits of himself he sets down his own existence, its bitterness, curiosity and love. Here are the elements that make this or that particular man different. He may be similar in many ways to a twin brother, but over a lifetime his peculiarly personal composition shows. Gevura is one life. For most of us it is the upper limit of a temporal appreciation. On the death of a parent the real grief is shorter than imagined. The presence of that person is soon forgotten, not out of disrespect, but in that life, your own life, goes on. Even for the surviving spouse, providing he does not retire out of life into memories, the chances are he will soon be considering marriage to fill up his last years. This is the sense of one life, the first and last breaths marked out by impressions, and seen through the screen of Yesod. The later years fly by as the once freshly tuned organism slows down and the ageing mechanism of the body seems to dull the senses and blurr the interior rhythms. However, Gevura belongs to the company of Tepheret and Hesed, the triad of self-consciousness, and as the years accumulate so should the awareness of the non-physical realm and its other-world time. Gevura and Hesed are the angels guarding the gates of Eden. It is possible to enter paradise even during the sojourn in the world of action and matter. In this way man is unique from the animals, in that on reaching his prime he can rise above the law of his body and carry on growing. Here he moves out of the physical laws of accident, into those of fate. If he can ascend higher up the central column he comes consciously under the hand of Destiny.

Hesed is the expansion of Time, in contrast to the contraction and differentiation of Time in Gevura. In this Sephira it is the power that extends beyond the life of an individual. In physical terms it is the life span of the species of a creature. In this Sephira are all men, at every age and time. Here is the dynamic behind a population explosion with millions upon millions of dead, as well as the thin slice of the living, inheriting the Earth. Hesed is the great impulse of the human race spreading out over the planet from its primal origins. It is a vast scale of time stretching over a million years. For us, we see it in the lives of previous generations, their achievements and work speaking of the human genius. Anyone who participates in this level of Time is in the least a historian, at most a great teacher founding a civilisation. This is the dimension we catch a glimpse of when we see the Acropolis or the pyramids; but more, it is the sense of countless lives all forming one being known as Man or, in Cabalistic terms, Adam.

Daat, as is to be guessed, is unique. It occupies, on the

central axis of consciousness, a special place. While the Sephiroth of the outer columns define functions, the central ones appertain to that creature's awareness. In Yesod is the mirror image of passing time made up of the feed-in from the other Sephiroth. This is a variable picture of Malcut, when looking down. When Tepheret is the focus as the watcher or observer (sometimes manifest, as said, in crises or accidents), Yesod becomes the obedient executive. Then Time ceases to just pass by and becomes, according to the need of Tepheret, attentive at the most useful level—in the case of an accident—in Netzah and Hod. With the added and culti-vated facilities of Gevura and Hesed, another dimension of Time is accessible. This is Daat, the door into Timelessness, as it allows the flow upward into Kether. This phenomenon is not the same as those memories of periods 'out of time' often felt in love affairs, but closer to profound religious experience upon which no clock, be it the 'now' of Hod or the cycle of Netzah, can be placed. Not even the glimpse of a life-time or the faint after-image of a distant epoch can be set in the same class. Daat is the edge of where Time does not exist.

Binah in physical terms is Nature. Included in its time-scale are all the living things of organic life. It dates from the first living molecular cell and terminates with the final breath of the last dying creature on our planet. It is, to us, this side of eternity. Still within grasp of understanding, we may grope with the problems of survival common to all living things. Our museums are full of bones and shells of long-dead beings so primitive that we are revolted by the violence they lived and died in, but we can at least appreciate the primitive desires of the prehistoric trilobate and dinosaur. We can look across a vast gap in time and view the various organic experiments, see the evolution of plants, insects, and animals. Even now, we can recognise a twenty-million-year-old footstep on a rock and trace ferns in coal, but when we come to stone without the sign of life, we stumble into another kind of time. Binah is Mother Nature, the receptacle of the creative impulse. She is the builder of prototypes, the designer of creatures and plants that are needed to clothe the Earth for a particular period. At the beginning, only simple organisms were needed to convert the incoming cosmic energy flow. Later the planet required more sensitive receptors, and Nature responded, eventually producing the body of man which could be inhabited by something more than vital force. Here was a new element added to the intelligence of the planet. Binah setting each one of her children to do a task, and working through the determinates of Gevura below, made sure the plants and animals lived their species' life within definite limits. Only man could free himself from her absolute rule, and that could only be by escape through one life at a time, out of the general law of the species, through Daat. For a man the Triad Binah, Hochma Tepheret is his destiny—with the knowledge of Daat he can open a door on to the Divine and escape the Wheel of Existence.

The time of Hochma on this scale is the planet. For a man it is far beyond his time, and yet he can perceive, in flashes of deep intellect, what the Earth's time measure might be like. He can work out, with clues given by rocks, samples from the moon, the periodicity of the planets and the vast cycles of the Sun, what the Earth perceives if it were conscious of itself. He can guess that with its surrounding protoplasm of air and radiation belts, it at least exhibits the most primitive cell-like resemblance of a living being: and with his knowledge of the microscopic realm that which appears to be dead and rigid is in fact in a high state of flux and even in osmosis exchange with space. The Earth, if it is alive, is not very old, and man knows by deduction and speculation that in relation to the Milky Way the solar system is less than middle-aged. On these time scales nothing has any personal meaning to man, any more than the truth that the remote galaxy of Andromeda seen today by us is in fact what it looked like several million years ago. These vast distances and times are only measurable in their own terms. The Sun to a man is eternal, but it is no more than a flicker to the Milky Way. The planet is for man the Hochma of his Time, the progenitor of Nature and his species. It is not, however long its immense life, Eternity, though in the relative world it may take on that name for an undeveloped man. Herein lies the strangeness of Time. A highly developed spiritual man may transfer himself into the next world, thereby side-stepping the usual hierarchy of age. He may, as has been said in many religions, be seen after physical death, and in some cases return to Earth in a time or period of his own choosing. This is only possible if he has risen up the column of consciousness, a unique and rare accomplishment among millions of human existences.

Kether is the Crown. In its hollow circlet is timelessness. Beyond and above is not even timelessness. From this Sephira issues that which is manifest as Time. Time is movement. Behind movement is stillness. Behind stillness, Nothing. Kether is the Crown, gateway out of the prison of even Eternity.

In relation to the four Worlds each Tree and Sephiroth has its own Time, though to the lower worlds it will be incommensurable, the upper world being no more than a presence, or possibility, like our view of life before birth or after death. It is impossible to explain our world's time in terms of another, but this does not preclude experience of it, or deny the miraculous when the upper realms manifest on our level of existence.

XVII

Planet Earth: a speculation

Shifting our scale, we move away from man into the Cosmos
of the Earth and using the Tree, this time as a telescope, we
examine and speculate on a larger order of Being than our
own. In an ancient philosophical system called the Doctrine
of the Cosmoses the various levels of a Universe are divided
up into a hierarchy of orders. In this, different worlds
are placed one to another, in a definite relationship. Thus
man fits within the Cosmos (the word means Order) of
Nature, which in turn is enclosed by the terrestrial Cosmos
of the planetary body. The Earth is itself part of a planetary system which is enveloped by the next level in the
Universe, that of the Sun. All stars are contained in turn by
the Cosmos of Nebulae, our particular one known as the
Milky Way. Beyond the Cosmos of all galaxies we can only
speculate.

Having defined a hierarchy of cosmoses we can, by placing
the Earth in the object glass, or Tepheret of our Cabalistic
telescope, see what composes the being of our planet, for
it is more than a mere solid ball enclosed by spheres of
water, gas, radiation, and life.

Beginning with Malcut we see the material ground base
of the Earth with its four elements or various states of matter.
These may be composed of all the elements known to science,
and of more yet to be discovered. This is the world we study
in geography and geology, but it is not the real Earth, any
more than the body of Christ taken down from the Cross

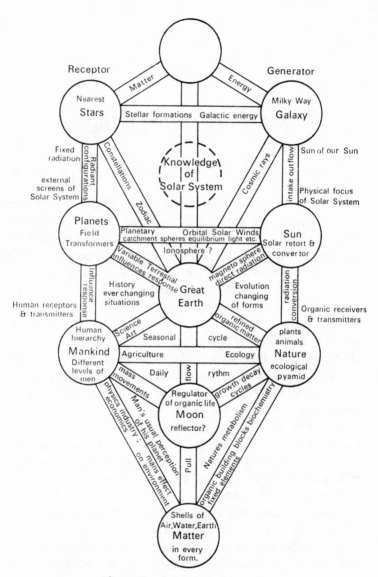

Planet Earth (speculative notes)

was the man himself. This is the core, the densest nodal point visible to our physical eyes, which only perceive surfaces. Malcut in this study is perhaps the most elusive aspect, for being ourselves embedded in it, we cannot always see our way out of it. Remember when we look up at the sky and see the Sun, Moon, and planets, even the Milky Way, we are in fact seeing the Malcut of those worlds. This must be borne in mind as we move up this particular Tree of Life. Each Sephira is an operating level, not just an astronomical object. A meditating man may appear, at a glance, to be doing nothing. But as with Buddha seated under his Bohdi Tree, this apparent physical inaction hid the cosmic activity of inner illumination.

The circling Moon in this scheme is Yesod and as previously said, the satellite is a giant pendulum, creating a tidal rhythm not only in the terrestrial seas, but in all the fluidic substances on the Earth's surface. Besides affecting the pulsation of growth, it pulls at all large fluidic masses, and this includes people. In its connection to Hod, or mankind in this context, Yesod for the Earth is the tidal motion of regular movements, be they the daily round of eating or the ebb and flow of a big city's rush hours. Yesod, in modern parlance, is the basis for mass statics. It governs the fixed cycles in man, en masse, through the Yesod-Hod path. The Yesod-Netzah path is easier to observe, with the pulse of Nature regulated throughout the year in conjunction with the Hesed or Sun, and the Tepheret of Earth, Netzah or Nature triad. Within the triad Nature, moon, and elements are many of the minor organic rhythms needed to maintain plants, animals, and men. The path Nature-Malcut relates to the building blocks of earth elements, and the biochemistry needed to work the cells and organs constructed. The Malcut-Yesod path designs are various organic body plans, with the Yesod-Netzah path governing their vitality. On the other side, the triad Hod, Yesod, Malcut describes the activities of man towards the physical aspect of the planet. The Hod- Malcut path is the study and utilisation of raw materials, be it for science, industry or building. Here is physics and economics, with human Yesodic power supplying the working engine.

Hod for the Earth is mankind. Men are the planet's voluntary processes. Moreover mankind is divided, like the senses and faculties we possess, into various functions. There are several theoretical divisions, but we shall take just three. Based on the body types, men fall into roughly the instinctive, emotional, or intellectual categories. These are extremely broad definitions, but they illustrate three sensors required by the planet. The instinctive section of humanity is concerned with action, the carrying out of work. Composing the majority, these are the people who do the practical tasks, and this can range from clearing a forest, farming, or industry, to the jobs of town planning, economics, and government. The emotional sector is much rarer, and these men are scattered throughout the world community as the heart of mankind. They are the receptors and creators of mood. Such people appear in religion and the arts, though they can emerge as leaders in time of war or act as emotional beacons in periods of peace. These are the poets, the artists, the men who reveal beauty in the midst of drudgery. They are the entertainers, the jokers, or the man who changes a quarrel into laughter. Emotion is vital to mankind. If it were not present man would be inhuman, and the Earth would suffer the ravages of continual war. If it were not for love of the beautiful, the good and truth, there would be no civilisation.

The intellectual section of mankind is smaller still. This does not include the café or university philosopher who competes with his peers for ascendency rather than the pursuit of wisdom. Here is a very rare circle of people made up of real thinkers who slowly, consciously raise and change the direction of mankind. From the view of the planet each of these types of men contributes to its evolution and understanding. Men by their labour refine the Earth, Malcut; and by their study add to the Earth more knowledge about itself. This is fed in along the Hod-Tepheret path. The more sensitive men become, the greater the planet's perception, so that when men split the atom or examine the Milky Way they are doing more than accumulating their own sum of information. With the growing world population this sensibility is increasing, and with mass communication the swiftness of the interchange of ideas multiplies. This creates a very interesting picture, especially as the sum total of mankind's Tree of Life (a complete Tree in every Sephira) is slowly filled out and developed. For the planet, the evolution of mankind is vital. The survival of man is also the Earth's concern. Here is the most sensitive organic apparatus the Earth possesses and the planet, like a man, will not allow itself to be paralysed, or go blind or deaf, without trying to stop it. The intelligence of the Earth is greater than man's, and no doubt the vast emigrations of the nineteenth century were part of a definite phase of growth in the planet's evolution. With the advent of a faint global consciousness, since men landed on the Moon, a new era for the Earth's knowledge of self-consciousness has begun.

Netzah is organic life. For the Earth it is all the vital round of the season's ebb and flow across the equator. Throughout the ecological pyramid the cycles in the chain of eaters and eaten convert the Sun, here in Hesed, and the four elements, into organic matter, which feeds and refines the planet's surface. Millenia of generations of plants and animals have coated the rocky surface and sea floor of the globe with humus and ooze. This is quite a different skin to the bare mineral core which, uncovered, would make it look like that embryo world, the moon. Nature absorbs the flux of active energy flowing from the solar Hesed and creates, with the Tepheret of the Earth, the triad of organic evolution. In response to Hod on the far side of the Tree it is controlled by man, who with his increasing knowledge of natural law practises the art of agriculture, improving some species of plants and animals and eliminating others. This could be likened to a man bringing his metabolism into better balance by applying an intelligent diet. Of course as in life, excess does happen and we pollute our system with bad management—even antibiotics. This however is corrected, though it may not be seen to be so for generations. A man who plants an orchard for his grandchildren to enjoy is part of this Hod-Netzah path. The Hod, Netzah, Yesod triad is also the daily round, but unlike the two side triads centred on Yesod, it is a relationship between the active and passive sides of the Tree. Here man is in unison with Nature and produces a healthy controlled environment. It is this triad most men exist. In balance, a pleasant and fertile environment; out of balance, a city slum, with only weeds and factory-farmed foods for nourishment.

The goddess of Netzah is Venus, and for the Earth she puts on the finest shows of grace and entertainment, continually changing her style each season, with plants, animals and men displaying their finery during courtship. In Netzah is natural love, and as the old song says, this makes the world go round. As accurate as any cliché this is the definition of Netzah-Eternity, that is, endlessly repeating. The Spring always comes after Winter, the birds come and go at the same time each year, the rains fall in the right season, and ripened fruits fall every Autumn. This is for the Earth the myriad reliable, repetitive processes. By these millions of interwoven lives blooming and withering, being born and dying, is the cellular skin of the planet created. Through this film, about ten miles thick from ocean floor to mountain peak, flow the elements, but raised by life to a higher state than mere solid, liquid, gas, and radiance. As Hod is the extension of the planet's sensibility so Netzah is that which not only gives our planet its strange exotic beauty, but makes it vibrant with the natural life of the biosphere.

Tepheret is the Earth itself. It is the being; focus of all the Sepheroth except Malcut. This creature is much larger than the stone ball we stand on, and it is made up of the infeed of all the Sephiroth. It contains the Hesed-Sun, in its radiant nature, though what it radiates we shall not know fully till we look back at it from deep space. It has the molecular makeup common to the planets, and no doubt partakes of the substance and energy of the distant stars. Nothing in the physical universe exists in a void. Space is filled with fine gas, streaming particles, winds of radiation, and even fragments of solid iron. The Earth, like a man, is not an island, it is part of the solar system and as such performs, within the Tree of Life of that cosmic organisation, a Sephirotic function. What this is shall be left for another investigation. The Tepheret of our particular planet is the beauty of its Tree. Quite different from Mars or Jupiter, its image in the heavens, as we know from space photographs, is breath-taking. To us Earth creatures this must be so, though no doubt if there are any beings on Mars their own planet's Tepheret would be equally beautiful.

Tepheret has direct connections with Gevura and Hod, and in this triad is seen the history of man. Here in human terms are the outer emotions and judgements, stimulated by the influence of Gevura or the planets on Hod, or mankind. At one time point the balance of stimulus might be tense, at another time lax, and from this we might suspect certain planetary combinations, like human feelings, might give rise to wars or periods of depression, as we have seen in the dark ages of man. Conversely the Gevuraic influence can create a renaissance, and in conjunction with other conditions a great religious movement, or an industrial or political revolution. The interaction of Hod, Gevura, and Tepheret (depending on which is active, which passive, and which conditioning), will produce an era of a particular character. This is mankind responding to the Earth's judgements, and like an individual, his outer reflexes reveal his mood. One might reckon the two world wars as a rather black one.

On the other side of the Earth's Tree we have the triad of Hesed, Tepheret, Netzah. This, as in man, is the vital processes. The Hesed Sun shines on to the Earth, but it cannot absorb such potent power readily. Some of this high-frequency energy has to be transformed by Nature into an acceptable form, and this particular triad is concerned with extending the range of Nature to accommodate the change in vibration, thus we get myriads of species of fauna and flora each one designed to absorb a wave band. Here also is birth and death, the cyclic process necessary to feed the Earth. While Nature lives off the elements, it in turn is eaten or absorbed by the planet in a literal osmosis, in that we find coal and oil seams deep below the surface of the earth. It is well known that worms cause unmaintained buildings to eventually disappear into the ground, not because they sink, but because all over the globe new soil is being created by dead organic matter; the worms, millions to an acre, complete the churning. The whole world, from the hardest rocks to the falling leaf, is in a state of flux. The Tepheret, Hesed, Netzah triad is this highly complex process. The round of seasons, apart from giving the Earth a new coat a year, grafts on a new ever-expanding skin, the topmost layer called the living.

Gevura is the other planets. From the view of the Earth the planets form a layered series of orbits, each one of quite different character. These in a space scale are the next largest Cosmos, and contain the Earth. On a planetary time measure, that is as the planets see themselves, the orbits are spiral tubes, one inside the other enclosing the luminous spine described by the moving Sun. This makes the Solar System appear like a sheathed firefly circling the Galaxy.

These planetary sheaths form an arrangement of limitations for our planet, which is confined within a narrow orbital belt. The significance of this is Gevuric in that the other planets act on the Earth as determinates of its incoming influences. This would imply that before reaching the Earth Stellar Binah and Solar Hesed radiation have to pass through the planetary fields first. As each planet has quite a different function in the Solar System, rather like body organs which select and reject the energy and matter passing through them, so it is with Earth at Tepheret. On this Tree, the planets act as the Earth's outer emotional judgement. A strange concept for us, but as said the history of mankind gives us some hint to the Earth's moods, so that if we regard the human race as the Hod Face features of the planet we see that it indeed does become angry periodically, and even smile sometimes as a craze like the Hula Hoop circuits the globe.

On this living Earth scheme one could assume that the interacting fields of the planets, not the solid cores seen through telescopes, do have an effect on the Earth. Besides the obvious example of gravitational pull there is probably much more passing between the planets than our scientists have yet detected. In the way that people affect each other, the myths of the gods describes very strong sympathies and antipathies between the planets. These exchanges and relationships, besides influencing humanity, also alter the balance of the Earth's invisible body, of which the atmosphere and magnetosphere are but the lower physical levels of a very tenuous and subtle mantle. Gevura is partner to the Hesed and Tepheret triad. This is the triad of self-consciousness. For the Earth this state is of a much higher order than the crude responses of Nature which are confined to the narrow law of the cell. By the same law of 'as above, so below' the planets are bound to the molecular and the Sun to the atomic world. Such worlds operate at a much faster and finer rate than organic processes. In these kingdoms cycles are both greater and smaller than man's general experience. However, he is in a unique position, in that he as the Microcosm is situated exactly half way between the upper and lower worlds and can participate in them because he is also composed of the same substance and energy, beside being modelled on the same pattern. The rare experience of real self-knowledge and illumination on the human level gives an insight into these realms. The Earth's awareness is undoubtedly very fine. This is the level in man of emotional intelligence through which, in ancient times it was said, it was possible to talk with the gods. Perhaps the gods still converse, and in the dialogue between the planets, take that radiance or nectar emitted by the Sun and pass it about amongst themselves. Gevura here is all the planets, and being below Binah, the stars, we can see by the triad formed with Tepheret that it relates the Earth to the constellations. In this triad is the constant, objective background of the nearer stars. Related to the pillar of Form the Earth's connection with this triad is destiny, as in man's Tree, in that while it is being fed by the Energy column, it is confined to a particular type of planetary life by its position within planetary and stellar worlds. This is the effect of Binah when the constitution of the solar system was first formed.

The Sun sits in the Sephira of Hesed. Receiving energy directly from the galaxy-Hochma, it also absorbs the emanations of the Lighting Flash, that is from Daat. Daat may be read (and we only speculate) as the knowledge of the entire solar system. The Sun is merely the focus of the organisation, its radiant body the hot-point pivot, like the heated core of our planet is the physical centre of the upper Earth. Into the Sun flows energy from the galactic field. The Sun also collects, along with this force, cosmic gas and dust which it converts by nuclear fission into radiation, but of a lower frequency than galactic emission. This is blown out into space from the Sun's visible body through the corona, to be caught by the planets, who, with their screening orbits, extract energy and substance each according to its nature. Here is Hesed and Gevura at work in the Sun's expansion and the planetary constraints. Our Earth, at Tepheret, in this Tree, circling millions of times about the Sun as it proceeds round the Galaxy, selects what she can catch, with Nature or Netzah lying just below Hesed fixing in her stomach of plants and animals, the nourishment of the Sun. This intake varies over the millenia, and Nature adapts accordingly, designing new species or modifying old ones to accept the change of quality and quantity. This point is well illustrated in the annual cycle by the fact that every flower has its particular time of year to bloom and will not, except under forced conditioning, open until then. Every bloom has its own colour, and we know scientifically that what we in fact see in red, yellow or any hue is but a rejected colour, the rest having been absorbed. This indicates that certain plants retain certain wave lengths of the solar radiation, and these are required on that part of the global surface at that point of the year. Over a long period this is the function of the Tepheret, Netzah, Hesed triad which has created plants, fish, insects, dinosaurs, and then mammals, to be able to absorb more Hesedic radiation. Man is in a strange position. Part animal and plant he can relate to the central column of consciousness, and thus bypass general evolution. This, however, is his individual choice.

The triad Hesed, Tepheret, Hochma we may only guess at. From Hochma, the Milky Way, comes the finest of cosmic radiations. These fine energy-particles penetrate the outer and inner Earth, and their arrival is vital to the planet's life for atomic, chemical and organic mutation. Without doubt the highly rarefied force field of the Galaxy is also present, rather like the Hochma equivalent in man, in the potent dynamic of Wisdom which can change the course of a life. For the Earth, Hochma is perhaps the profound omnipotence of the Milky Way which is the progenitor of its existence. In the triad of Earth, Sun and Galaxy is great power, with Hochma feeding Hesed and Tepheret from the creative level of the physical Universe.

The Sun is a point of interchange between force and form. It is the most obvious evidence to ordinary men of cosmic action. Here in Hesed is an abundance of incandescent energy and matter blasting out in every direction. Massive beyond the imagination's grasp the Sun is impossible to look upon without darkened glasses, such is its power. Without the vital input of the Sun, organic Life, and the Earth, indeed all the planets, would die. Our closest example and representative of the Stellar world of Binah, the Sun is the dynamic manifestation of Hesed, directly beneath the super-power of the Milky Way of Hochma.

Daat, that mysterious Sephira of Knowledge, can be no more than a hazarded guess in this speculation. Lying on the axis of consciousness it aligns with the Will of the Creator. This gives us a clue to its nature. Placed in the centre of the triad Hochma, Binah, Tepheret, it appears to be the cosmic consciousness of the Solar System. Here is perhaps the Earth's inherent knowledge of its origin. Situated beneath the Supernal Mother and Father it could be the point of conception for the Solar Sytem, the Earth being a vital organ in that cosmic organism. At Daat, under the Will of the Absolute, the Active and Passive forces, working through the Universe of Action and Elements, generate motion, or Time, and the receptive stillness of Space, from which emerge the various worlds we have been examining. Above all these, at the apex of the Divine triad, resides Kether the Crown, which reaching down through the Sephiroth passes eventually into Malcut, the Bridge, hidden in the virgin elements of the Universe. Here She waits for her Bridegroom's coming, to return either by way of slow evolution, or directly up through the conscious Column of Equilibrium.

XVIII

Man

By now our study of the Tree of Life should have brought
us at least to the stage of familiarity with its terms, and
through the examples examined some idea of how it
functions. To know all this may be academically satisfying
and we can go on examining everything beneath the Sun
for ever, without coming to any real understanding. This is
not the aim of the Tree. As its name implies it must be rooted
in Life. No Tree is complete without Kether reaching down
to Malcut. If the Lightning Flash does not reach the ground
there is no Tree, Heaven is not manifest in Earth. It is the
function of man to assist this to happen.

Man is a complete Tree of Life. In him is the potential for
its full realisation. Though in his normal state he merely
exists, the Sephiroth are present with most of the paths and
triads ticking over. This is our position. Let us then briefly
review the situation before seeing what can be done to bring
the Crown to the Kingdom.

We will have observed during our study that in the case
of man the passive column is the receptor, not only to the
inner Sephiroth but also to the outer aspect of a man.
Through Binah, Gevura and Hod, he perceives the world in
form, while the inner Sephiroth—Hochma, Hesed, and Netzah—define a dynamic core, which, though hardly ever seen,
nevertheless drives our being. These inner and outer aspects
are the active and passive poles which the column of equilibrium keeps in balance, besides giving us consciousness.

This arrangement operates throughout the four divisions of a man represented in the Assiatic, Yetziratic, Briatic and Atziluthic levels of the Tree; or in more human terms, the physical, emotional, intellectual and spiritual aspects of his nature.

Taking the physical level first, we define this zone by the great triad Netzah, Hod, Malcut with Yesod in its centre. Here we can describe the sub-triads roughly as follows: Hod, Yesod, Malcut deal with external impressions, with the path between Hod and Yesod filing and screening data; the Hod-Malcut Path, the physical senses and controls, through the nervous system; while the middle Yesod-Malcut Path relates to the man's image of his body, which would include all those acquired poses of his personality. This triad might also be called 'Comparisons'.

The Yesod, Netzah, Malcut triad could be named as 'Internal Impressions'. Here the path between Yesod and Netzah is concerned with the vitality level expressed in daily states, also with personal habits. The Netzah-Malcut path describes the body mechanism and its maintenance. These are the elements in a biochemical system. The Yesod-Malcut path, marrying with the Hod factor, gives the body its energy to make the expressions and movements being carried out by face and limbs. Above these two side triads is the Hod, Netzah, Yesod triangle. This is the zone of inter-action between the voluntary and autonomic processes. The Hod-Netzah path demonstrates this well with a blend of instinctive and trained reflexes. These are stored in the brain and can, when needed, be circulated either way round this vegetable principle triad, through Yesod. During sleep, dreams—often a discharge of tension in one of the Sephiroth —are displayed on the screen of Yesod. In the case of madness the lower triads, as in sleep, just maintain open lines, while imaginary activities take place in the almost detached triad of this physical triangle. The Hod, Netzah, Yesod con-

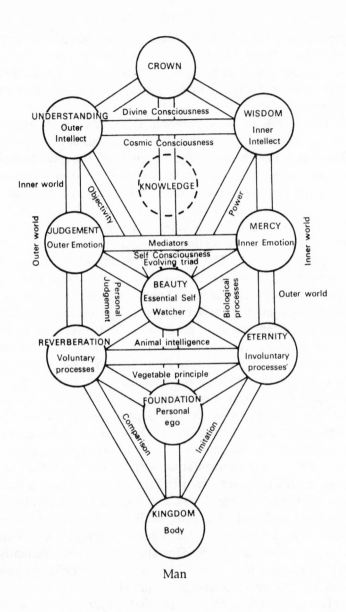

Man

figuration is, as said, vegetable in nature, being principally concerned with life support. This, contrary to common belief, does not include the basic ingredients of real intellect and emotion found in man. Life can go on without these higher faculties.

The next level to be reviewed is the triad Hod, Netzah, Tepheret. This can be called the animal soul or intelligence, the Nefesh in Cabalistic terminology. With the great triangle below, it completes the working part of Adam, or mankind. This triad is part of the emotional world and gives man access to the Yetziratic universe of forms. The apex of the animal pyramid is Tepheret. Here is a man's individual self, or the Watcher, sometimes recognised as the impartial observer of events. This is when the shift of consciousness moves up from its normal ego focus in the image world of Yesod, into the clear eye of Apollo, who sees with his Sun vision right into the darkest corner. This central self of a man is his judgement seat or direct access point to every part of the Tree except Malcut and Kether. The lower Face, or Natural man, formed by Tepheret, Hod, Netzah, and Malcut, is shielded by the mask of the Yesodic persona from an un-bearable confrontation with the world as it actually is, until he can face it, whereas the Superior man, formed by Tepheret, Binah, Hochma and Kether, has the upper central point of Daat as the gate of Void, or Knowledge to seal from or make a direct confrontation with God, Whom, the Bible says, no man has seen face to face and lived. In this well-protected context the Essential Nature is a seed planted in the body and soul of a man, until it is ready to fructify. Meanwhile he has to live and move amongst his fellows. This the lower part of the Tree allows him to do efficiently, which enables him to perform his natural tasks without waking up from his delusions too quickly.

The triad formed by Gevura, Hod, Tepheret being of an outer emotional nature can be called personal judgements.

A look at the connecting paths will quickly explain this when one sees how data collected by Hod, related emotionally through Gevura to Tepheret, cannot be other than self orientated. The subdivisions are self-study, valued judgements, and even anger, depending on which way the triad flow is initiated.

On the opposite side of this emotional box formed by Gevura, Hesed, Netzah and Hod is the triad Tepheret, Hesed, Netzah, with the human parallels of inner emotion, self, and instinct. This is a very creative series of processes, ranging from the making of love to the practice of great art. Here is a powerful system pouring energy down into the body and into the ego. This also can have its good or bad manifestations if it is not corrected by the constraints coming from the other side of the Tree. The path Netzah-Tepheret could become profligate without the control of Hod. Generally speaking the Hesed-Tepheret path carries a deep sense of well-being, and this tempers the sense of ego with a feeling of something bigger than oneself. This is a state often found in religious experience. The Hesed-Netzah path is related to life, death, and biological generation.

The upper triad of this emotional aspect of a man, composed of Gevura, Hesed and Tepheret, defines the evolving part of a human being. Here is the beginning of self-consciousness, as against just being conscious as any animal is. This triad is, with the back-up of the triads below, able to have a balanced assessment of itself. Centred on the Essential Nature the consciousness can call on both inner and outer emotion, Judgement and Mercy, to view its actions. It is sometimes called conscience. Here in the Yetzeratic World the Neshuma is a crystallisation of a man's soul. It is possible, it is said, to form here a Yetzeratic body of a subtler substance than elemental materiality which probably conforms more closely to what a man is really like. In life we meet people whose ego-personality masks their inner nature from us, and sometimes even from themselves. Occasionally, for example, we get the feeling that perhaps a very beautiful woman is not so beautiful inside, or that an apparently dull exterior hides a profound man. This is a glimpse of the Yetzeratic or psychological world. (Perceptive painters and writers use this Gevura, Hesed, Tepheret triad, with its extraordinary sensibility, to give us pentetrating works of art.) However, though this invisible aspect of our nature exists, it can grow or shrivel, become good or evilly inclined, lean to the left or right side of the Tree and become unbalanced by tending towards a harsh ever-judging temperament or an ever-tolerant, over-indulgent attitude. In spiritual work it is manifest on the left of the Tree by the puritan zealot, on the right by the undiscriminating saint. This triad, as can be seen, is the beginning of evolution for man. With its paths he can have determination and charity, make tempered judgements, and receive encouragement from a deep inner resource. With his Essential Nature at the pivot of so many paths and lying on the axis of consciousness, his awareness in the invisible realm of emotion is cultivated, and a door to the upper world of true intellect is opened.

What we normally consider as intellect is in fact Hod. In life the use of words, our memory bank and world picture stored in Yesod, all go to make up what is generally called mind. Most modern clinical psychology deals with this area, which is strictly mechanics. Statistics, psychological tests and the vast array of laboratory conclusions all demonstrate the mechanicalness of the lower mind centred on Yesod. Any attempt by these techniques to analyse art, real thought, or mystical ecstasy fails miserably, especially when conducted by observers who do not accept non-rational experience, except as an aberration. Experiments on rats and samples of population may prove the animal likeness of social patterns, but when it comes to individual analysis it takes a trained but intuitive psychologist, or better still an artist like Rembrandt or a writer of Tolstoy's calibre, to describe someone else's inner nature really accurately.

Real intellect is rare. Certainly thousands of books have been written and lectures given with an intellectual flavour, but these belong to Hod, the Sephira of learning, and scholarship is not intellect. Outer intellect is Binah—Understanding. This is the result of a deep and long pondering, though its results may manifest in a flash conclusion with the aid of Hochma—Wisdom. The triad formed by Outer Intellect, Outer Emotion and the Essential Nature will give impersonal judgements, while on the other side of the Tree the triad, composed of the Inner Intellect, Inner Emotion, and the Essential Nature, will create a vision given to few men. The paths of these two side triads, with a little study, explain themselves. The outer triad is the definition, in emotional form, of the conclusions made by Binah to Tepheret; and the inner, the inspiration perceived by Tepheret, and derived from the illumination of Hochma in conjunction with Hesed.

Of the central triad formed by outer and inner intellect and the Essential Nature little can be said from personal experience. This is the triad of Cosmic Consciousness, that is, an objective view of the Universe as it really is. Down the path Binah to Tepheret is Law and Righteousness, and down the other, headed by Hochma, Illumination and Recognition. Across the top lies the Binah-Hochma path with the initiator and the receptor principles. Knowledge and loss of 'I' in the vastness of the Cosmic void manifests at the centre of this triangle of the Spirit. This is the World of Creations. If a man obtains access to this realm he is already preparing to pass out through Daat into the Supernal kingdom of Emanations.

Above the intellectual level in a man is the Divine triad.

Here is the Causal World, always in existence, yet hidden. Here also is the presence of the Absolute at the Crown of the column of consciousness. Situated at the apex of the Mother and Father triad, Kether is the entry point into the Relative Universe of the Will of the Absolute, which passing down through the spirit, then the soul, enters the physical organism composed of the four elements of Malcut. This extraordinary creature is man—that is, you.

XIX

Aim

One might ask what is the aim of all this learning? What indeed is the point in living? To any considering person it is apparent that Life is a learning situation. The intelligent accept this quickly and do not repeat obvious contraventions of law, whether they are man-made or natural. Most people come into contact with spiritual law via their upbringing or in the customs of their society, but this is often mere imitation of an outer practice, the shell of something deeper, that has long been forgotten. This can be said of all religions which only keep the letter of the law. For anyone who wishes to progress further than merely following the outward practice of his father, he can look at his own particular tradition and see, if it is a complete one, that there is an inner content that is common to all religions. This usually gives very clear directions on the problems of living.

It would appear that from conception to birth we descend into the physical realm, and then by the passage of time return on death to another kingdom. However, it does not follow that we grow as individuals; though our bodies may mature perfectly as far as Nature is concerned, she is interested only in a planetary purpose. For us, as individuals, we have choice. We can travel the biological path, fulfilling our organic commitment to set the next generation going, only to die, like the mayfly after breeding; or we can grow as souls. Every man and woman has this possibility, and for those who do not take it one can only speculate on the

various traditional views that they will return again and
again. For the rest, the small number who do wish to grow,
the teaching and learning situation presented by life becomes fascinating.

Anyone who realises that everything learned is not necessarily related to ego, status, or possessions, quickly recognises their own personal position is precisely a reflection of
their inner state. They will also see that whatever happens
to them, whether it appears good or bad at first sight, is
specifically designed for their benefit. Having already removed themselves from the law of accident this may be
thought of as fate, that is, related to one's type, but it is not.
Once a man begins to understand his situation, that is,
arrives at the triad of self-consciousness, he begins to alter
the mechanical nature of his life and the fatal pattern of his
existence. From this point on he has the possibility of
Destiny, that is the release from the general laws governing
men. By developing himself and accepting the Absolute's
Will he can begin to move through life seeing it as a vast
cosmic drama in which he is literally an actor. The chief
difference is that he knows his role, and can see, when he is
from time to time awake in his Tepheret, what and what not
to do in every circumstance. At this point he comes into more
and more contact with his Spirit. Here he may be chosen to
carry out some particular task. This is destiny. While performing this cosmic job, under Will, perhaps for other
individuals or even the planet itself, he will be led, as the
Aladdin story tells, out of the chamber of copper and silver
and through the chamber of gold, that is bright cosmic intellect. Here he can view the creative processes behind the
forms that mould the Physical Universe. Beyond this lies the
last room of himself wherein hangs the magic lamp, and
who did not as a child wish to find such a treasure?.

This is the most practical use of the Tree. Apart from
studying other organisms and organisations we should reflect

on its relation to ourselves and its application to our
lives.

All men begin, at birth, in the great bottom triangle of
Hod, Netzah, Malcut, with Yesod in the middle. However,
centred on Yesod are three minor triads, and these, depending on the particular emphasis in a man, manifesting through
the predominant activity of the fore, mid or hind brains,
place him in one of the three major divisions of the human
race, that is of the head, heart and gut body type. As said
in the chapter on Earth, the vast majority of people are
instinctive, and it must be clearly understood that the terms
intellectual, emotional, and instinctive, as used in ordinary
life, mostly relate to this bottom physical major triad. So
that a man with the predominance of the Hod, Yesod, Malcut
triangle is what is usually called an intellectual, that is to
say, he has a good working cerebrum. The Netzah, Yesod,
Malcut emphasis is the body-orientated or instinctive man
for obvious reasons, and the Hod, Netzah, Yesod person is
often regarded as emotional in that he tends to respond
initially through feeling. None of these divisions are superior
to each other. They are all in a state of mechanical cycling
in relation to the rest of a Tree. A man may have the potential of a great thinker, poet, or explorer, but unawakened he
is as all other dreamers. These types are defined 'Waking-
sleepers', or men numbers 1, 2, and 3. They are all quite
equal on this level.

The moment a man begins to be aware of himself, he
enters into the upper Hod, Netzah, Tepheret triad. From
here he can, and usually does, slip back into the routine of
life and into the Yesodic world of the physical ego mind. If
he sustains the effort, he may in time gain access to that yet
higher triad which is already faintly existent in himself, of
Gevura, Hesed, Tepheret, that is, Self Consciousness. This
makes available new powers which feed his awakening soul.
The quickening of these two triads of Awakening Conscious-

ness and Self Consciousness, centred on his Essential Nature, are marks of evolving men and are numbered 4 and 5 respectively. To the man who has reached this point on the Tree many possibilities open. He is standing at the zenith position of his earthly existence and can look out and below to the Natural World with discrimination and charity, or above and inwards to the Supernatural, without having to leave the physical Universe.

If, with Grace, he should become man 6 he would have reached a situation where he could perform miracles. In Christian terms such a man stands in the position of the Son, at Tepheret, with the Father at Kether, and the Holy Ghost between them at Daat. Blessed with the Holy Spirit of Knowledge he can obtain the highest level of a man and become absorbed in the Divine, having thereby returned from whence he came. These are the great ones of Mankind, helping Eve the soul and Adam the embodied Spirit to regain Paradise and Heaven.

This then is our aim, for the Tree of Life is a conscious ladder by which man can reach his Maker. He may climb up the left column by complete submission, or the right by complete freedom. Both of these ways require great effort and discipline. The simplest way is up the centre column of equilibrium, which does not require utter obedience or total licence, whose ways and methods are fraught each with their own kind of temptation and difficulties. The central column is a different matter. Being concerned with consciousness rather than function a man can receive help straight from Heaven. All that is needed is practice and a fine sense of balance. Looking neither to left nor right such a person can draw on both sides of the Tree and rise up step by step through the central triads, using life itself to fill out his experience of the inner and outer, the above and below, till in the fullness of his time he returns home.

The Tree of Life is an analogue of the Absolute, the Uni-

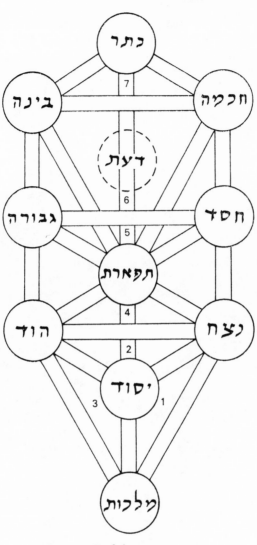

Evolving man

verse and Man. Its roots penetrate deep into the earth below and its top branches touch the uppermost heaven.

Man, meeting point between heaven and earth, is an image of his Creator. A complete, but unrealised Tree in miniature, and lower than the angels, his is to choose to rise higher by climbing the branches of himself and so gaining the Ultimate Fruit.

Appendix

The *Tree of Life* (or *Introduction to the Cabala*) was first published sixteen years ago and during those years I have continued to learn about this subject. Many of my new findings have been written about in subsequent books, but I think it right to add an appendix to this "Introduction" in order to enlarge its scope and indicate the greater depths of the Cabala. As an example, the anatomy of the psyche is examined relating modern psychology to the ancient system of Cabala. (See the figure on pg. 198.) In this comparison we shall see the development of the study.

Taking Malcut as the body composed of the four states of matter we can observe how it perceives the Physical World through the central nervous system via the five senses. Also from the body come the instinctive drives of the Id or Nefesh, the vital soul. These divide into the libido and mortido principles of life and death that are crucial to survival at the physical level. Hod and Netzah, the active and passive Sephiroth, are the bio-psycho processes of receptivity and initiation on the liminal threshold between body and psyche. They form, with Malcut, the great triad of Action, Thought, and Feeling, with ordinary Ego mind at the centre. This is the pivot of the sphere of personal consciousness that takes in impressions from the outer world and holds the balance of the pre-conscious — that is, what can be recalled from memory. Here, too, is the identity of the personality — the mask adopted as the social role of the individual. The Shadow, or unacceptable darker aspect that can cut the individual off from the Self at Tepheret is also found here.

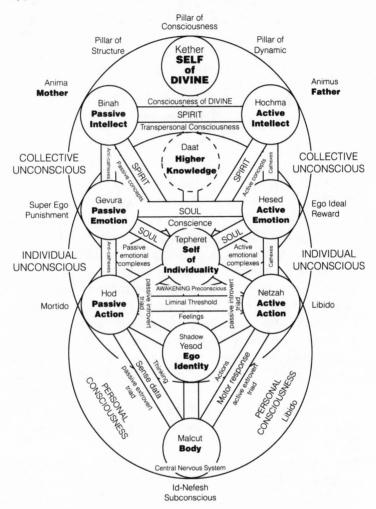

Figure 22. The Tree of Life. Here the psyche is set out upon the Tree which is the key diagram of Cabala. The notations place various aspects of the psyche at different levels within their functions. The interactions and penetrations of these factors generate structure and dynamics, as well as the degrees of consciousness and unconsciousness.

The Self is the central coordinator of the psyche and the place of what one really is, be it Beauty or Beast. Just below the Self is the triad of Awakening, where moments of insight and clarity are experienced. The two side triads contained by Tepheret, Yesod, Hod, and Netzah are introverted by nature, while the lower triad of Thinking and Action are predominantly extroverted. Here are the four functions of Jung that influence the Ego. The whole of the lower face, as it is called, is all most people are aware of. That which lies above and beyond ordinary consciousness is the Unconscious.

The side triads associated with Gevura-Hod, Hesed-Netzah, Binah-Gevura, and Hochma-Hesed, centred on Tepheret, relate to the emotional and intellectual complexes. Those on the right stimulate action such as enthusiasm and creativity, while those on the left are concerned with holding a steadying balance with their content of emotional restraint and rules of life. These side triads are built up of both individual and collective experience so that there is a blend on the left of what one should not do, in contrast to the right which allows and indeed encourages one to do. Modern psychology calls the left side the Super Ego and the right the Ego Ideal. These punish and reward according to the values of society and the individual's unconscious, which is governed by the structural and dynamic character of the psyche. The inner voice of an absent parent is often an expression of the Super Ego and Ego Ideal warning or supporting some thought, feeling, or action.

When individuation begins to occur, that is, as a person starts to be himself or herself at Tepheret, versus the roles he or she may act out in the Ego or Yesod, then there is a battle between the tribal level of the Super-Ego-Ideal and the soul (or the triad Tepheret-Gevura-Hesed). Here is the place of free will, in contrast to the reflexes of the individual unconscious. Self or Tepheret consciousness enables the individual to perceive life as a whole and as one capable of consciously working out fate, instead of being pushed and pulled by parental opinion and tribal custom. Thus the son of a miner will leave his village and become an artist and the daughter of a stockbroker will live in a remote forest in order to be herself. This is only possible when the soul is more powerful than the unconscious forces of the Super–Ego–Ideal.

The great triad of the Spirit formed by Binah–Tepheret–Hochma represents the transpersonal level. This is the place where cosmic consciousness resides deep in the psyche. It connects the individual with the collective mind of the community and the whole of humanity. Thus a person may have the values of a Moslem and yet have much in common with a Hindu or Jew at the basic level of being part of mankind. Here the great archetypes of Mother and Father and Anima and Animus are shared by all. They are universal, which is the quality and dimension of this triad. In most people, this level is totally unconscious, although he or she lives by its dictates every day. For example, in time of war a nation rallies to the flag in defense of freedom, the party, or a faith, and millions join up to fight others equally subject to the same pressure. The ephemeral tides of fashion – as well as the more enduring ways of religion – all operate through the collective mind to govern most of humanity. It must also be said that this is the place where the great saints and sages receive their mystic experience through the Non–Sephira of Daat or Higher Knowledge. This grants them the gift of prophecy and illumination as well as an objective and universal view of the world.

The topmost triad formed by Binah–Kether–Hochma is the psyche's connection with the Divine. Here the individual can experience, in deep meditation, or through an act of Grace coming down the central column, the presence of the SELF or the Holy One. Such moments are not as rare as imagined, as the Tree of the psyche is designed in such a way that contact with the highest World of Atziluth is possible. This gives access to Eternity that many mystics and ordinary people, in a moment of illumination, during perhaps a quite mundane event, speak of.

At such a moment, Time becomes one as the person perceives everything in the past, present and future through the realisation of the Eternal Now.

The four Worlds of Atziluth (Emanation), Briah (Creation), Yetzirah (Formation), and Assiah (Action) are present within the single Tree of the psyche, which is basically Yetziratic by nature. What this suggests and is confirmed by further investigation in both experience and the Tradition, is that there are four interpenetrating Trees which form a Jacob's Ladder of all Existence. These are joined by overlapping so that the Kether of Briah comes out of the Tepheret of Atziluth, while the Kether of Yetzirah emerges from the Tepheret of Briah. The Crown of the Tree of Assiah comes forth from the Tepheret of Yetzirah which forms a chain of interlinked worlds that some Cabalists call the Great Tree. The ten Sephiroth, plus the Non-Sephira of Daat, when placed upon the central column, make up a vertical axis of consciousness running through every level of Existence. This is discussed in great detail in later books.

Looking at the psyche as a whole, one realises that it is a system of checks and balances from below and above and from side to side. In the case of madness or extreme pressure, one side can be predominant, producing depression on the left, or mania on the right. Likewise, an excessive materialistic emphasis in the lower area can curtail the growth of the soul and the spirit, while the reverse will generate a delusion that believes the inner world is more important than outer reality. The function of the Yesod–Ego is to facilitate the interaction between the conscious and unconscious and this it also does through dreams, the workings of the mind. Some dreams or unconscious expressions, such as Freudian slips of the tongue or peculiar gestures can indicate, for example, impulses that have been repressed into the side triads of Emotion and Intellect. They may also be manifestations of the Super–Ego–Ideal that will reveal guilt or approval through strange moods or by giving gifts to someone who may not know whether the gift is an insult or a compliment.

There are many subtle and complex processes in the psyche in everyday life as well as in the progression of development. Thus a person can move from identification with the body to an inflation of the Yesodic Ego when he or she gets a very good job! Likewise Hod or Netzah can be over or underactive, and Gevura and Hesed finely balanced if the individual knows what his or her capacity and limits are. An excessive Hochma can generate genius, but without a checking Binah it can lead to insanity, which is the dislocation of the Tree when Tepheret can no longer coordinate it. Normally the slight or great variations of growth and crisis are coped with by the Self that monitors everything through the paths and triads that focus upon it, so that a set back or advance is controlled and no great disruption occurs. Like the body, the psyche is, on a whole, well run. It only becomes sick if there is a chronic imbalance or an acute situation. Most times the psyche has its own solutions. If not, then the counsellor or analyst acts as the Tepheret until the balance of mind is again resolved.

The Tree of Life has many more dimensions than are at first apparent. The paths, triads and Sephiroth make up a simple yet highly diverse system by which one can analyse any organism. By contemplating the Tree and knowing its components well, one can gain access to every level and function of a given subject. It gives us insights into how we may apply the method and so penetrate deeper into the object being contemplated, as well as the Grand Design upon which all Existence is based. The rabbis have said that the reason for Existence is that it acts as a vast mirror of contemplation by which God may behold God. Our effort to comprehend the meaning and purpose of ourselves and the world is but part of a vast plan that is unfolding through our individual lives as well as in the life of the Universe.

The Self that is in us is that same SELF within all. Our reflection is the reponse to the highest and first Name of God I AM THAT I AM. In this Work of Self realisation, the Holy One beholds the Holy One through our experience.

Index